John Holme Burrow

Jabez Oliphant

The Modern Prince; Vol. 3

John Holme Burrow

Jabez Oliphant
The Modern Prince; Vol. 3

ISBN/EAN: 9783337053604

Printed in Europe, USA, Canada, Australia, Japan

Cover: Foto ©Andreas Hilbeck / pixelio.de

More available books at **www.hansebooks.com**

JABEZ OLIPHANT;

OR,

THE MODERN PRINCE.

A Novel.

IN THREE VOLUMES.
VOL. III.

LONDON:

RICHARD BENTLEY, NEW BURLINGTON STREET,

Publisher in Ordinary to Her Majesty.

1870.

CONTENTS OF VOL. III.

BOOK IV.—*continued.*

BOOK THE LAST.—THE PRINCE IN RE-TIREMENT.

JABEZ OLIPHANT.

CHAPTER V.

THE TRIUMVIRATE.

WHEN the ladies had left the dining room at the Hall and the wine had gone round pretty freely, Mr. Oliphant informed Sir George Highside and Truman what the business was for which he desired their assistance. This was to consider what course it would now be best to take with regard to John Hawtrey, whose enormities in having placed himself on the same sofa with Mrs. Mansfield and in refusing to give up his visits to that lady at Mr. Oliphant's demand, he specified with much particularity. He also kindly detailed the whole of the correspondence which had passed between the schoolmaster and himself.

"Sly dog, Hawtrey ! eh, Oliphant ?" was the baronet's chuckling comment when the story was finished. Sir George was by this time purple in the face and his utterance rather thick ; but his after-dinner allowance of port always made him more jovial and less dignified. " Wonder he hasn't better taste, though. She's fifteen years older than I am, and as plain,—why, as Truman, there."

Jabez was considerably displeased at the levity with which the baronet, who had been a sinner himself, spoke of the matter : " This affair is one of great importance, Sir George," he said. " I consider it a public reproach which ought without delay to be removed from amongst us ; and as friendly expostulations have no effect, it is plainly necessary to take severer measures. Can you suggest anything, Mr. Truman ?"

"Well, I don't think such things are much in my line," answered the parson with *naïve* simplicity. "If it had been a working man, you see, Mr. Oliphant, one could have gone to him and reasoned with him, but to a respectable person like Hawtrey — pooh, *no* clergyman would do it."

"You hit a blot there, sir, in the universal conduct of your profession," said Mr. Oliphant, with grave satire ; "I quite agree with you that there is scarcely a clergyman living who would have the moral courage to say the same things to a rich man which he says to the poor every day, though the faults were exactly the same ; and it looks as though you think there is one morality for the rich and another for the poor. But

in this case I do not think remonstrances
would do any good; I have tried them
myself, you see, and have failed."

" All this must be very unpleasant to Mrs.
Mansfield, poor body, when one thinks what
she has had to go through," remarked Joseph.

" It is very unpleasant to all of us—
duties generally are.   But the question is,
what are we to do ?"

" That puzzles me, I'm sure," answered
the parson, not liking to say point-blank that
he did not wish to meddle with the business.

" Then can you help us, Sir George ?"

" Eh, what ?" asked the baronet.

" Can you advise us what to do next in
this matter ?"

" Do ! why, shake hands and be friends,
man.   That's what I say; that's the Highside style, Oliphant,—always was.   Pooh,
pooh, man ; never mind a bit of a shindy—
ink's cheap—so's paper—never mind—

shake hands and be friends,—good friends all round, eh ?"

" Excuse me, Sir George, but you make a great mistake if you regard this as a mere personal quarrel," replied Jabez. " Mr. Hawtrey may either be my friend, or he may be my enemy—it is immaterial to me or the question. I take my stand on higher ground : his immoral conduct is a scandal to society, a disgrace to his cloth, and a gross example to his pupils ; and I am determined he shall be punished."

" Yes, yes, shake hands and be friends," Highside repeated jollily. " You're good fellow, Oliphant,—good dinner,—good wine, —only thing is you don't drink. Hawtrey's good fellow too ; shake hands and be friends."

Mr. Oliphant turned with a little anger from the slightly inebriated baronet to his other guest.

" Well, Mr. Truman, if you have not yet hit on any plan, I should like to mention the one which has occurred to myself, and which, after much reading and deep thought, I am convinced will prove to be the best."

Jabez here cleared his throat with a loud hem, his usual note of preparation, at which ominous sound Sir George instinctively made a dive at the bottle, and the parson leaned back in his chair with a look of pious resignation. On the present occasion, however, Mr. Oliphant's speech was short.

" Gentlemen," he said, with firmness and solemnity, " Mr. Hawtrey must be EXCOMMUNICATED."

The parson, in his amazement, leaped up from his chair so suddenly as to upset his wine-glass : " Good God, Mr. Oliphant, are you mad ?" he exclaimed.

" No, Mr Truman, neither mad, nor even

labouring under any unusual excitement," answered Jabez, replacing the glass with a courteous smile. "I knew you would think it a strong measure, but I believe it to be our only way out of the difficulty, as I will show you, if you will kindly sit down again."

The parson sat down again, with surprise still on his face. As for the baronet, his little pig's eyes were glaring at Mr. Oliphant in helpless bewilderment.

"Yes, I am quite aware," continued Jabez, "that excommunication is an extreme punishment, gentlemen; but is not this an extreme case? Consider, what you both admit, the enormity of the offence, aggravated by its long continuance, by his stubborn refusal to amend his conduct, and by his position. Consider next the vast and wide-spreading injury that such a vice, if not speedily rooted out with a strong hand, will do to the community at large : crimes are like diseases—some are more contagious than others, and the more contagious they are, the more energetic should be the remedies employed. If Mr. Hawtrey goes unpunished or insufficiently punished, well known as he is from his position, and known as his conduct therefore must be to so many, will not all his acquaintance think they have *carte blanche* to commit any act of immorality they like without fear? Add the difficulty of finding other means of punishment, a difficulty which you just now confessed yourselves unequal to solve, and I think you will own that if I can prove the applicability of excommunication, this is the only remedy that is left us.

"Now I find that immorality such as Hawtrey's has ever been looked upon both by the canonical and statute law as a spiritual

offence most properly appertaining to ecclesiastical jurisdiction. For instance" (Mr.
Oliphant here got down an armful of old
books, and after laying them on the table,
handed one to Truman), "there you will
see that in 13 Edw. I. stat. 4, 'adultery
and such like' are called 'such things as
be mere spiritual,' and therefore are treated
as things to be punished by spiritual courts
alone. Again, look at the 109th Canon,
where the churchwardens are required to
present to their ordinaries any persons who
offend their brethren by uncleanness and
wickedness of life, that they may be punished according to their deserts. In many
of the other Canons you will find the same
principle more or less clearly laid down.
But in the case of a clerk in holy orders
like Hawtrey, the point is even more
strongly insisted on, for the church seems
always jealously to have guarded her right

of correcting her own ministers ; I will only ask you, for example, to look at Canon 57, where you see that 'ministers ought to excel all others in purity of life—under pain of ecclesiastical censures to be inflicted with severity.'

" The offence, then, being a spiritual one, done by an ecclesiastic, and belonging specially to the ecclesiastical courts, what punishment is so suitable as excommunication, which is a purely ecclesiastical censure ? Then, again, it is pleasant to think that, as Blackstone says in this passage, we should be adopting the plan of the spiritual courts and be punishing the criminal not by way of revenge, but *pro salute animæ*, for the safety of the offender's soul alone, which I always hold to be the only true principle of all legal severity.   The only objections, I think, which you can possibly urge against excommunication, are two,—

that it is a remedy which has dropped into lamentable disuse, and that no further consequences would be attached to it in the present state of the law. But I answer that if it is a rare punishment, it is all the more likely to be striking and effective; and that, as to the second objection, we ought not, perhaps, to be *too* severe till we see whether there is any chance of reforming the delinquent, at which no one would rejoice more than myself."

By this time Joseph had rallied his senses, and he hit one blot out of many in Mr. Oliphant's reasoning. "Your arguments, Mr. Oliphant," he said, "are very good no doubt, and you know a deal more about excommunication than I do : but— but I don't quite see that we have any proof whatever that John Hawtrey is guilty of the offence, and you cannot get a man condemned without proof."

" Proof !   And what do you call proof ?
He does not even dare to deny his guilt ;
he actually says with utter shamelessness
in one of his letters that 'I may draw
what inferences I please :' and if a man
will not plead, the court must necessarily
conclude him guilty."

" Nay, he might dispute the jurisdiction
of the court," observed the parson slily.

" A public man, sir, like the challenger
at a tournament, is bound to enter the lists
whoever touches his shield," answered
Jabez.   " And even if these visits are innocent, which I do not think, Hawtrey is now
well aware in what light they are viewed,
and by obstinately refusing to discontinue
them, is responsible for all the injurious
effects they may have.   A man in office
must give up even his most harmless amusement if it clashes in the popular belief with
his duties.   Mr. Hawtrey will not do this,

and I must again press on you the impera-
tive necessity of excommunicating him."

."On *me*, Mr. Oliphant!—why, bless my
soul, you don't mean that I am the man to
excommunicate him?"

"Certainly you are the proper person,
Mr. Truman," replied Jabez, with a winning smile, "and the only person, if, as I
could wish, the censure is to be pronounced
quickly and without a great deal of trouble
in the present state of the law—without citing him before the bishop, in fact.
Mr. Hawtrey is one of your own parishioners, and excommunication seems to me to
be quite within the province of either a rural
dean or a surrogate—both which offices I
need not say we have all much pleasure in
seeing combined in yourself, my dear sir.
Do help yourself to another glass of
port."

"But surrogate—rural dean! Good

gracious, I never dreamed of anything of this kind : I always thought a surrogate had nothing to do but with wills and so on ; and as to a rural dean—why, bless me, I didn't know that he had anything in the world to do !"

" Oh, but you must not under-estimate your own powers and prerogatives, Mr. Truman. If you will be kind enough to turn to the 382nd page there" (Jabez blandly gave him the open volume), " you will find that a rural dean is a deputy of the bishop and, having to inspect the conduct of the clergy around, is armed with an inferior degree of judicial and coercive authority, which would surely extend so far as the mere pronouncing a decree of excommunication. So a surrogate, as you will see here—from his being the substitute of a bishop or a bishop's chancellor."

The parson gave a long whistle of despair.

Knowing happily nothing about ecclesiastical censures himself, he took for granted what was thus boldly asserted, namely, that as rural dean or surrogate he had a right to excommunicate notorious offenders in his parish. No doubt he thought it very odd indeed that, if he had such a power, he should never have heard of its existence before ; and he felt certain it could only be based on some obsolete but unrepealed enactment which Jabez had fished out of the abyss of forgotten laws. Still it did not even occur to him to doubt the accuracy of a statement of Mr. Oliphant, whose truthfulness and high sense of honour he knew. The fact was, however, that Jabez, having *begun* his researches with the profound conviction that excommunication by the incumbent was the only proper punishment for Hawtrey, and *must* be found to be legal, had so bewildered himself by hunting this ecclesiastical prerogative through the forests and jungles of the Statutes at Large and a wilderness of folios—tracking it out through labyrinths of " whereas-es," " furthermores" and " notwithstandings," through canons and conventions and decretals,—and after all only to find it alternately a spiritual will-o'-the-wisp and a contumacious beast with claws, catch sight of it here in the plain charge of a bluff bishop and lose it there behind the mailed glove of a king, or run it down as he thought in a precedent and then, presto ! see it bolt under an Act of Parliament just as he laid his hands on it—he was so bewildered, I say, with all this that he had failed to perceive how decently and completely the middle-age hobgoblin he was in search of had been laid to rest for ever by modern statutes.   Or perhaps in these statutes he saw loop-holes which ordinary minds do not

see: one cannot tell; one can only be sure
that the judgment at which he arrived
was honest, however much mistaken it
might be.

But poor Truman did not even know that
Mr. Oliphant was probably mistaken, and
he felt cold drops of perspiration on his
forehead, so great was the dilemma in which
he conceived himself placed; for he had
quite made up his mind already that it was
impossible to do what Mr. Oliphant wished,
and yet that gentleman, who had been so
munificent to him, would be mortally
offended if he declined to comply.

"But John Hawtrey is a very intimate
friend of mine, Mr. Oliphant," said Joseph
at last, with the air of a drowning man
catching at a straw.

"Yes, my dear sir, that will certainly
make it more painful," replied Jabez, pluck-
ing the straw away. "He was a friend of

mine also, and I can sympathise with your feelings. But you remember the philosopher's magnificent dictum that his friend was dear but truth dearer still? Justice is an inexorable goddess; to her we must sacrifice, if occasion calls, our property, our friendships, nay, our lives themselves."

"Well, but really, Mr. Oliphant, I don't know anything whatever about the process of excommunication — never did such a thing in my life—never dreamed of it, bless you!"

"I anticipated that objection, Mr. Truman," said Jabez with pitiless courtesy, "and have taken the trouble to look out the proper form from the authorities on the subject. You will find it in these volumes which I will lend you; if you peruse them, never fear but you will do your duty admirably."

The parson groaned. "I must have time

to think the thing over," he said: "one can't decide in such a hurry what to do."

"Certainly: it will do if you let me know your decision in a few days, though to my own mind the case appears as clear as possible.—I hope, Sir George, you will join me in urging our friend here to do his duty strenuously, however unpleasant it may be. I am sure from your long silence that you thoroughly agree with me this course is the only one left us."

"No, no, by Gad, no!" exclaimed the baronet, as if waking from a dream. "John Hawtrey's good fellow—went to school to him: so did you, Oliphant. Mustn't be excommunicated—oh, no!"

"I am much surprised, Sir George, that you should allow your private feelings to influence you on such an important matter; and you a magistrate!" said Mr. Oliphant.

"Ah, very well: but he mustn't be excommunicated. Has good blood in his veins, has Hawtrey, though his father was poor."

"I do not see," answered Jabez, in considerable wrath at this Balaam who had been brought to curse and had blessed instead, "why good blood as you call it, should give a man a privilege to commit any offence he pleases."

"Mustn't be excommunicated," repeated the baronet, more positively. "Highsides stand by him."

"Then you must allow me to tell you that in spite of all the Highsides he shall be excommunicated, as justice requires," cried Mr. Oliphant in flaming anger.

Sir George was not so intoxicated as not to be still touchy about his dignity when it was assailed. He jumped up and rang the bell to order his carriage, muttering, " impudent fellow — son of a cobbler — tea-dealer!" all which expressions Mr. Oliphant unluckily overheard and never forgave. Not forgetting however that the baronet was a guest, he bowed him out to his carriage with even more than ordinary courtesy; but they did not shake hands on parting, and Jabez returned to the dining-room if possible more exasperated against the representative of the Highsides than against the schoolmaster. Truman did not stay long after this explosion, but all he would say in answer to Mr. Oliphant's pressing him again to excommunicate Hawtrey, was that "he would think of it."

Soon afterwards Lord Stainmore arrived, and he was cosily sipping his tea by the drawing-room fire with Mr. and Mrs. Oliphant, when the door was rather hastily opened, and Kate, followed by Holden, swept into the apartment.

CHAPTER VI.

JUSTICE.

THE drawing-room at the Hall was so large and long that, to make it more cosy during the winter evenings, a tall screen in the shape of a quarter of a circle was usually extended from one side of the fire-place halfway across the apartment. Jabez and Mrs. Oliphant were now seated within the snug space which was thus partitioned off, and were both facing the fire; while Lord Stainmore was in an easy chair at the other side and therefore a little beyond the screen, in the more open part of the room. Mr. Oliphant was never fond of glare, and a couple of wax candles on the mantelpiece were the only light in addition to the unsteady blaze of the fire. Thus the whole of the room, except the small enclosed space, was wrapped in that dim and flickering twilight in which everything is visible but nothing distinct, and which is so favourable to grotesque tricks of the imagination.

When Miss Oliphant and her companion arrived at the door, which was on the same side as the screen but a considerable distance down the room, she left Frank to advance up the apartment more leisurely, and hurried forward, partly in her excitement, and partly to prepare her uncle for the artist's extraordinary reappearance. Accordingly she swept, as I said, past the end of the curtained area, and throwing her arms round the neck of her uncle, who was nearest her, kissed him, exclaiming in clear decisive tones, "Uncle, you love justice, and I am come for it."

Very beautiful she looked as she stood erect the next instant, with heightened colour and sparkling eyes, waiting for his answer.

" My dear Kate, you shall have it—if it is anything I can do. What can you mean ?" returned Jabez with a look of astonishment in which he was joined by the two others. Stainmore however, recovering from his surprise, was rising from his chair with his blandest smile to welcome her, when he caught sight of Holden who had now advanced nearly to the end of the screen but was visible to him alone.

Never was there change in a man so instantaneous. The smile vanished and he stood transfixed with fright and horror, his hair almost bristling and his face becoming first deadly pale and then absolutely livid as he glared at the grey figure in the dim light before him. So great was the shock

that all consciousness of those in whose presence he was seemed to have passed away
for the time.

"Ah—here? Merciful heaven! then
they were not dreams," he exclaimed in a
low terror-struck voice that electrified every-
one with its earnestness. "What do you
want now? Blood! it is always more blood!
—I thought I told you it was Carlo."

The artist, rather enjoying the other's
fright, advanced a step or two more in
silence, though still not so far as to become
visible to Mr. and Mrs. Oliphant. On this
an expression of still deeper terror, if possible, fixed itself on the viscount's face and
he stepped hastily behind his chair, with
his eyes still fastened on Holden, and almost shrieked out, "Come no nearer! I
am not to be frightened—I will not give it,
I tell you—no nearer!"

So quickly had all this passed, and so

amazed were the spectators, that Kate only now found power to say to her uncle, "Uncle, Mr. Holden is still living, and has come with me. Are you not ashamed of yourself, my lord?"

Mr. Oliphant now perceived Frank, and rising gave him a stately but most cordial grasp of the hand: "Bless me, Mr. Holden, I little expected to have the pleasure of seeing you again! It is truly wonderful how we can have been deceived so much; but we are delighted to welcome you back to Reinsber."

"Thank you, Mr. Oliphant," replied Frank, "but I fear my news is scarcely worth a welcome."

"No? Well, we will hear you and decide. You know Lord Stainmore, I think. Your arrival or something seems to have agitated him in a very unusual manner: I cannot quite understand it yet."

Stainmore had now in some measure regained his self-possession, though, having been quite delirious for the time, he was unconscious how far he had committed himself. On Kate's announcement that Holden was still living, he pressed his hand on his brows and his face became flushed with shame. Accustomed however to disguise or control his feelings, he now came forward, though his voice still trembled with agitation.

"I think I have been ill," he said; "my head is strangely light. Your coming on us so suddenly, Holden—I hope I—I did nothing—I said nothing to—that is, to startle you?"

"You thought Mr. Holden a ghost; that was all," said Miss Oliphant, with cold contempt.

"A ghost! Ha, ha,—that was good. Well, then, I was certainly a great fool,

Kate," he replied with an affected laugh. "Pray excuse me. I have always been dreadfully afraid of ghosts. It was an old nurse who used to frighten me when quite a child with such stories, and I have never quite got over them. Ha, ha! A—a very wrong thing of the nurse, Mr. Oliphant?"

"Perhaps your conscience had something to do with the matter on this occasion, my lord: I certainly do not envy you your dreams," remarked Kate.—"I believe you now, Frank,—every word."

"My conscience, Kate!" replied Stainmore. "Surely, you are giving me rather hard measure; but if I must make a full confession, this affair of Mr. Holden's, after my anxiety and exertions on his behalf, left such a deep impression on my mind that— I never told you before, I think? Well, one does not like to acknowledge one's weaknesses—but it positively haunted me for months, and I used to dream about him and think his spirit came to see me in my sleep, to urge me on to justice against his murderers. It was ridiculous enough, but surely, Kate, you will not doubt my courage for a trifle like this?"

"I do not doubt, my lord, that you have courage enough for anything bad, and presence of mind for any hypocrisy," said Kate.

"Well, I see I am in disgrace somehow. However, Mr. Holden, allow me to offer you my warmest congratulations on your escape." He advanced to Holden with out-stretched hand, but the artist only made him a cold bow.

"This is all very mysterious, Kate," said Mr. Oliphant, severely, "and I think you ought to explain at once what you mean. Lord Stainmore's fright under the circum-stances was very natural, and I do not know what the effect of Mr. Holden's sudden reappearance might have been even on myself if you had not prefaced it with the announcement that he was no ghost."

"I will explain myself, dearest uncle, and shall conceal nothing," replied his niece. "I told you that I came for justice, and it is justice on Mrs. Oliphant and Lord Stainmore there."

"Mrs. Oliphant and Lord Stainmore? This is surely a dream, too. However, speak on boldly, Kate: I will take care that full justice is done." And Jabez seated himself in an imposing judicial attitude, while the two culprits also sat listening intently, without saying a word.

Most girls would have shrunk from the ordeal of mentioning a deep-seated attachment before so large an audience, but Kate had much of her uncle's determination, and, being quite resolved that he should now know everything, did not flinch from her purpose. In few words but without the slightest hesitation, she related, as a preface to her story, the accidental way in which she and Frank, before the latter's departure from Reinsber, had discovered their attachment to one another; their fear of Mr. Oliphant's anger, yet their intention of asking his consent at once; and Mrs. Oliphant's promised intercession at the first possible opportunity, a promise in which they trusted, "and which," added Kate with a scornful glance at that silent lady, "she has so nobly fulfilled." Then, as she observed a look of deep pain and reproach on her uncle's face, her courage gave way for a minute or two, and she fell on her knees before him, clasping his hands and kissing them through her tears.

"I know I was wrong, dearest uncle," she said. "I ought never, never to have accepted Mr. Holden's offer till you knew it. But I was an ignorant girl carried away by the impulse of the moment, and we loved one another—oh so truly! Uncle, have you not loved, yourself?—I was sure of it; then will you not forgive me—your own Kate who never meant to deceive you? Say you forgive me."

"But I think Mr. Holden at any rate did not act very honourably in not making his avowal to me first," said Jabez. "I should be sorry to judge him harshly, but it *looks* like an abuse of my confidence, as if he had taken advantage of his position deliberately to steal your affections."

Holden coloured and exclaimed earnestly, "Indeed, indeed, Mr. Oliphant, you will do me great injustice if you think so. I was accidentally surprised into the avowal, as Miss Oliphant told you. When I first found out the state of my own feelings.

respecting her, I not only struggled with them, but was intending to leave Reinsber without giving the slightest hint of them to any one, and at the first moment I could stir after my illness."

"But did you think it right to leave the house without telling me what had passed?"

"That was not Mr. Holden's fault but mine, uncle," said Kate : "he was most anxious to tell you immediately, but I dissuaded him—trusting, as I said, to Mrs. Oliphant."

"Well, I do not think Mr. Holden acted in this case with *quite* his usual frankness —he ought to have insisted. However all men make mistakes sometimes, and we are under great obligations to him. As for you, Kate," he added, kissing her affectionately, "you were somewhat in fault too; but I know too well how good a girl you are, not to forgive you a childish attachment which has come to nothing.　Now go on with your story."

Though she did not like the ominous way in which he spoke of her affection for Holden, Miss Oliphant kissed her uncle again gratefully and rose.　She then informed him briefly of the correspondence between herself and Frank.　"Thus our engagement was a very short one," she said; "for neither Frank nor myself could bear the thought of its continuing longer when you were in ignorance of it.　Afterwards therefore we corresponded merely as friends."

"I am glad you repented of your error so soon, Kate: that was quite right," said Jabez, his face brightening.　"We shall always of course consider Mr. Holden a friend of the family.—Will you not sit down, Mr. Holden?"

Miss Oliphant continued: "I now come to the day when we heard from Lord Stainmore of Mr. Holden's disappearance. That was, if you remember, the 10th of December. On the 12th, Mrs. Oliphant—in fulfilment no doubt of her promise of assistance—wrote Mr. Holden this letter, enclosing the one which I now hand you and which purports to be from myself. Both are heartless falsehoods, for you will recollect that I was not engaged to Lord Stainmore till six months afterwards; but the one with my name attached is a forgery: I never wrote or dreamed of such a letter. Please read them and judge for yourself—oh, Mrs. Oliphant, how could you do it?"

Jabez took the letters with an exclamation of astonishment, and read them twice very carefully, his face growing sterner and sterner every minute.

"This is certainly Mrs. Oliphant's writing," he said at last in a tone of horror and wonder; "and as she refers to the other note, which seems an imitation of your hand, Kate, we may fairly conclude that she is responsible also for the second. But I can see no reason for her sending these notes under any circumstances, still less to a man she supposed dead."

"Might she not think, sir," said Holden, "that there was still a chance of my being found alive, and yet wish by these means to put a stop to my suit for ever? There is no doubt that, though professedly our friend, she was always at heart against the match."

"That is certainly a possible explanation and the only one I can see," replied Jabez. "Mrs. Oliphant, what have you to say about these vile documents?"

Mrs. Oliphant had been trying to coin a lie which would pass, but was unable to strike one off with the speed which the emergency required. She remained silent therefore till Jabez in an angry tone repeated the question.

" I knew you would not approve of such a *mésalliance,*" she said faintly at last.

" If I did not approve of it, at all events I would not have resorted to lying and forgery to stop it. Then you do not deny you wrote these letters—will you not speak ?"

"I wrote them," she replied, as before : " but I did it for the best, as——"

" Very well, Mrs. Oliphant," interrupted Jabez in awful tones. " You own the fact and that is enough. I have never liked you : I knew you to be mean and disingenuous, but I did not imagine I had been living so long by the side of such a sink of infamy as this. For the future you and I must part. You will leave Reinsber the first thing to-morrow morning and choose another home. I shall allow you a small annuity, providing nothing of this kind occurs again.”

“ Would it not be better to wait till to-morrow before deciding on the matter ?” asked Stainmore deferentially, as the wretched woman buried her face in her hands and began crying.

“ My lord, I trust I know my own business best,” replied Jabez.

“ Yes, uncle,” said Kate, “ and his lordship may soon find he has enough to do to attend to his own.”

“ Well, let us hear, Miss Oliphant,” replied Stainmore ; “ you speak so charmingly, I could listen for hours, whatever the subject.”

Kate tossed her head scornfully and, turning to Frank, asked him to finish the story. Holden, therefore, briefly narrated the particulars of his escape and the information he had obtained regarding the viscount's complicity in the attempt on his life. At the end he handed to Mr. Oliphant the documentary proofs he had brought with him, Carlo's deposition and others.

Mr. Oliphant took the papers and glanced over them, Stainmore leaning back in his chair the while with an easy smiling nonchalance. Presently Jabez hemmed and gave judgment.

" These papers, Mr. Holden, seem to be genuine documents, but really I do not see in them any proof of Lord Stainmore's connection in any way with this affair. In fact, the depositions themselves would not be admitted as evidence for a moment in their present form in a court of justice. But even if we admit them, what do they amount to ? Just to this—that a ruffian, Carlo, whose word no one could trust, deposes that a certain Englishman, named

Smythe, employed him to kill you and that
Lord Stainmore was in Naples at the time
under that very common name. No; you have
jumped to a monstrous and unwarrantable
conclusion : but if it is any satisfaction to
you, I may say, without vanity, that I am
a pretty good judge of character, and that
I have never met a more excellent, kind,
or generous man than this young nobleman.—You will excuse my having looked
at these papers, Stainmore," he added, with
a smile, " but I wished thoroughly to dis-
abuse Mr. Holden's mind of this strange
delusion ; it is always so unpleasant to see
an intelligent man the victim of a crotchet :
I could tell you some very amusing stories
about the extraordinary fancies of men I
have come across."

" Some other time, Oliphant, I hope to
hear them," said the viscount, smiling courteously, but with slight hauteur.   " Mr.

Holden's craze is certainly an amusing one : still, as he is a friend of yours and Kate's, I must thank you for trying so well to dispel it ; and with that object I will myself take the trouble to suggest that, English names being so monstrously difficult to foreigners, this Carlo, or what you call him, may very probably have been mistaken in the name of the Englishman who employed him, if he was employed. Besides, really, Mr. Holden," he continued, after a glance at Mrs. Oliphant to see if she were likely to take any part in the conversation, " what motive could I possibly have for killing you ? You and Miss Oliphant had kept your little affair quite secret, so that I could not be jealous of you, even if I had been in love with her at that time : just imagine the absurdity of a British peer making away, all for nothing, with a land-scape painter ! You do not seem to have heard of the trouble I gave myself about finding you—and I think it is rather hard, Kate, that you have not told him."

" Nor does Lord Stainmore seem to think that we have eyes or ears," retorted Kate. " Why were you so frightened when you saw Mr. Holden ?—Why did you talk of his ghost wanting more blood from you ?— Why did you speak of Carlo if you did not know him ?"

Mr. Oliphant came to the rescue : "Kate, you seem strangely prejudiced against your affianced husband just now. His lordship amply explained all this ; he said he had been subject to dreams about this affair from his very anxiety to assist Mr. Holden, and that from a boy he had been afraid of ghosts.—I will discuss that question with you, some time, of the proper education of children, Stainmore : it is a very important subject."

" Yes, uncle, but Carlo's name ?"

" Well, I rather think," replied Stainmore, " some Carlo was strongly suspected at the time, and perhaps the name might get mixed up with my dreams—I really can't say—you cannot expect one to remember everything that happens in dreams. —Now, is this queer mistake all explained ? Come, then, Mr. Holden, there is my hand —as a Christian, I forgive you your unkind suspicions with all my heart."

Mr. Oliphant said, " You are a very excellent young man, Stainmore ;" but Frank haughtily declined the hand, and Kate turned away in disgust from this specimen of a forgiving Christian. From her new point of view every word of the viscount's increased her prejudice against him.

Stainmore observed the action, but scarcely displayed his usual prudence in addressing her again at that moment :

"What, are you too still suspicious of me, Kate? I am entirely innocent, and you will be sorry for this to-morrow."

"That morrow will be long in coming, my lord," she answered.

"And yet a few hours ago you could love me?"

"Oh, even a few minutes work miracles of change—surely your dreams must have taught you that."

"Faith," exclaimed the viscount, turning to Mr. Oliphant in despair, "this looks unpropitious for the event on Saturday," the day fixed for the wedding.

"No, no," answered Jabez, aside; "the Oliphants do not break their engagements. This is merely a girlish prejudice, conceived in a moment and over as soon: I will reason with her, and you will see by a little tact we shall soon make her fonder of you than ever, as is the case, I believe, in all true lovers' quarrels, eh ?—Well, Kate, I know you are not quite yourself with all this, but you must perceive, on reflection, that you have spoken most unjustly to Lord Stainmore. You must remember that you are to be his wife to-morrow week."

" I am quite myself, dear uncle ; but his wife—never !"

" Pooh, pooh, Kate. You loved him and engaged yourself to him, and, as nothing whatever has occurred which can reasonably alter your opinion of him, we must keep our word."

" Nay, uncle, it is sometimes more wicked to keep one's word than to break it ; and this is not the man I pledged myself to : I pledged myself, as I thought, to an honest man, Frank's friend and yours ; this is Frank's enemy and—I will not say what besides."

" It is most absurd and wrong to persist

in this way, Kate, and I shall be very angry with you soon. You came here, as you said, for justice ;—did you find me remiss in doing you justice in Mrs. Oliphant's case where the proofs were clear? Well, I have carefully examined your allegations against Lord Stainmore also, and the justice you seek compels me to say that he is completely innocent."

"But you must pardon me, uncle, if, in a matter so nearly affecting myself, I have come to a different conclusion on the same evidence."

"You had no business, then, to come to a different conclusion," returned Jabez, angrily. "I can have no one's interest so nearly at heart as yours, and I have had far greater experience than yourself in the judgment of difficult cases. What, a raw girl! It is simply insolence and ingratitude not to defer at once."

"In almost everything, uncle, I would gladly, most gladly, defer to you ; and you have never found me backward, I trust, in rendering homage to your far greater intellect and experience. But sometimes (I do not know how, but I am sure it is so) woman's wit sees clearer than man's wisdom—and, though I am deeply sorry if I pain you by saying so, I cannot marry him ; I would sooner die."

"This is utter rebellion. Kate, Kate, I have been to you as a father."

"You have been more to me than a father," said Kate, kneeling again and bathing his hand with tears. "Dearest uncle, you gave me a father's love when I had not a daughter's claim. You took me from orphanage, sorrow, and poverty ; you fed me, clothed me, taught me ; and I learned neither least nor last how much true nobility I had to reverence in yourself.

In return—it was all I had—I have given you a daughter's love. Dear father, let me be your daughter still. Let me stay with you—I have no other wish now, and you would be very lonely without me. I will never marry and we will forget all this. If any old dream of love should ever trouble me, I will either crush it down, or say to it that you have done so much for me you are worthy of all the affection this poor little breast can give. We were very happy before by ourselves; we may surely be happy again."

"This is all very well, Kate; but I never did break my word in my life and I never will. I am astonished that you do not see how unjust and unreasonable your objections are. You must certainly marry him—you can then live at Reinsber as much as you like, if you and he can agree on the point; I need not say how happy

I should be to have you both with me still."

"On this point only, dear uncle, you must excuse my compliance."

"But I will not excuse you," rejoined Mr. Oliphant more angrily than ever. "You compel me to use my paternal authority, and I command you—mark—on pain of my very utmost displeasure, to promise you will marry him."

"Never, uncle," exclaimed Kate rising, "unless you could first make me love him, which you know very well you can no more do than you can command flame from heaven. Love comes only where love likes—wilfully, like the flowers ; and, when it does come, what has it to do with laws or authority, except to laugh at them ? Yet is it not holy, too ? I think so. I think the parent who steps between a girl and her choice questions a warrant every bit as valid as his own—he sets God's command against God's gift; and woe be to him if he does this unnecessarily or thoughtlessly, from some miserable election of his own or from mean motives of power, policy, or ambition. Still, since you object, I will not marry where I choose—but my own father should not make me marry where I do not choose."

"Indeed! And this is my dutiful niece Kate! What next, I wonder? Perhaps Miss Oliphant will even object to my reminding her that I have other relatives."

"And what of that, uncle?" asked Kate.

"What of that, presumptuous disobedient girl! I will not leave you a penny, not one penny, if you do not take his hand and promise to marry him instantly—instantly, do you hear?" cried Jabez, almost choking with fury.

Kate flushed indignantly and replied:

" I did not think, uncle, however angry you were, you would have insulted me. Your money indeed! I *will* not marry him."

" Leave the house, then; I will have no resistance to my authority here. Go— marry any beggar you choose—you can take your choice now. Ungrateful, inso- lent hussy! I will find a hundred to love me better than ever you have done, though you were so cunning in pretending it. Go —go—don't plague me with the sight of you any longer."

" To-night, uncle!" said Kate falteringly ; it was bitterly cold, and a storm of sleet and snow shook the windows. " Oh, you cannot be so cruel! Where am I to go ?"

" To the devil if you like. Ha! ha! I have touched you now, have I ? To-night ! this instant!"

" You could not be so unjust, surely, Mr.

Oliphant," cried Frank, with difficulty controlling his indignation.

"Who dares to say that I am unjust? And—and, d—n it, sir, what have *you* to do with the matter?"

"I have this to do with it, that, as an honest man, I must say you have not the vestige of a right—and you know it in your own heart—to compel Miss Oliphant to marry a man she does not like; and if you turn her out of doors on such a night, everybody will cry shame on you."

"Sir, I do not think you have acted so honourably yourself that you are entitled to lecture others. She would be the more valuable prize for yourself, I suppose, if she stopped," said Mr. Oliphant bitterly.

"Ay," echoed Lord Stainmore with a sarcastic laugh.

"You can think what you please about that," retorted Frank; "but I really must decline to take my code of honour either from an angry man or a would-be assassin."

" Well, sir," replied Stainmore, white with anger, " we shall meet again, I trust."

" The sooner the better," said the artist ; " I will then teach you a few lessons you greatly need, my lord."

" Very well, sir, very well," replied his lordship.

" But I trust our meeting will be face to face this time," Frank added contemptuously, " not a coward's stab in the dark."

" I will not have my guest insulted in my own house, Mr. Holden," broke in Mr. Oliphant. " I must beg you to leave it immediately ; I will be master here. And you, you most ungrateful girl, what are you stopping for ? Go—go instantly."

" Not to-night, I pray you, Oliphant," said Stainmore ; " she will see her mistake soon. Think what a night——"

"I will go now," said Kate haughtily. "Mr. Holden, will it be too much trouble to escort me down to the village? Then I will just get my hat again and meet you in the hall. Good-bye, then, dear uncle, and an orphan's thanks for all your kindness. You are angry now and have mistaken me —it is no matter—I trust you *will* find those who can give you better affection— and I am very sorry to pain you so much— and—it may be very long before we see each other again—do not let us part alto- gether in anger." And she approached as if to kiss him.

"No—no—you are no relative of mine now. Go and starve! your fate be on your own head. Don't write—don't come here again—I shall know you are only after my money." The exasperated old man struck at her with any insinuation which he thought would wound her.

Her lip quivered a little, but she answered kindly, "Then I will not trouble you, uncle, and so—farewell." Then she walked with a quiet but firm step across the room, and closed the door gently as usual.

After she and Holden were gone, Jabez sat a long time in silence looking gloomily into the fire, neither Stainmore nor Mrs. Oliphant daring to interrupt his meditations. At last he turned to the viscount with a long sigh.

"I must apologise to you, my lord," he said courteously, but with a trembling voice, "for your having been subjected to so much rudeness and such a breach of faith in my house. I am very sorry, but of course you see that nothing could be more against my own wish."

"Do not mention it, Mr. Oliphant," answered Stainmore; "I regret very deeply that I am the innocent cause of all this."

"Well, I am a victim equally with your-self to this gross defiance of authority."

"I hope, Mr. Oliphant," Mrs. Oliphant ventured by and by to say, "you have now reconsidered your determination about me. You see now for yourself what your niece is, how wilful, how infatuated with low society, and how——"

"Mrs. Oliphant," interrupted Jabez with a fresh burst of anger, "I have not recon-sidered my determination about you, be-cause it needs no reconsidering. That, at any rate, was just. You and your shameful duplicity are the real cause of all this, and if you say another word, by G—d, you shall go to-night, stormy as it is, like—like her."

Mrs. Oliphant slunk away to her room, crying; and Jabez rang the bell furiously to order in wine and cigars. He very rarely indulged in either, but to-night he both smoked and drank fiercely; and Stainmore, for companionship, filled his own glass and lighted a cigar.

"Till to-night," said Jabez, "I never thought myself such an old man as I am. Over sixty, one finds a very little excitement too much for one."

"To-night would have tried the strongest," replied Stainmore.

"Yes, yes. I had suffered her to wind herself about me too much, somehow."

"Ah, it does not pay to like anything too well. When you lose it the pain is far greater than any pleasure you ever had from it. Give me slight attachments and plenty of them : then, if you are unlucky in some, you do not care—you have scores as good, to fall back on. I always back the field against the favourite."

"It must have been because she was so like my brother," said Jabez, not noticing the other's maxim. "Poor John! it is as well he did not live to see this day. Such ingratitude, such unreasonable obstinacy !"

"You have certainly been very kind to her."

"Kind ! Yes. She was a little wild thing without a penny when I took her, and I gave her the very best education without any regard to expense, and I let her do almost what she liked—too much so, it seems. You would hardly believe it, but I allowed her three hundred a-year for pocket-money alone—three hundred pounds, my lord, each year—and paid all her bills besides. Ah me ! I know the time when I should have thought myself as rich as Crœsus if I had received half that amount for my whole salary—I really do not know which is happier, the shopman or the millionaire."

The other, not knowing how to console him, or not willing to take the trouble, let the old man ramble on till he asked nervously after a pause :

"I suppose you think I was right, my lord, in what I did ? I am rather stunned and my judgment is scarcely so clear as usual. But psha! I was right; paternal authority must be maintained at all costs."

Stainmore was glad that he was not required to answer the question, which would have put him in the dilemma either of offending Jabez by opposing him, or of confirming the old man in his resolution of throwing his niece off altogether. Neither of these alternatives suited the viscount, who was busy calculating the chances of a reconciliation between the two relatives, of course with a view to the great Stainmore interest therein.

"But you don't think," he answered, " that she will abandon you altogether, in this way ? Surely she will come back in the morning to ask your forgiveness—or soon at any rate ?"

"Do you really think so ?" said Jabez eagerly. "But she must agree to the marriage : I cannot honourably allow that to be broken off."

"I have been frequently to-night on the point of asking you to let me withdraw from the engagement, but I thought you might be annoyed at such a proposition, and perhaps might think I was backing out of an agreement unfairly. Of course to give her up would be a great grief and trial to me, but, sooner than cause such unhappiness, I think I ought to make the sacrifice." After Mr. Oliphant's last observation, the viscount thought he could air his generosity without cost.

"It is not to be thought of, Stainmore," replied the old man. "I will not allow you to suffer for the faults of my family if I can help it. Your offer is a very noble one, but do not speak of it again, or you will offend me. If she ever comes back to Reinsber, she shall come on condition of restoring the honour of our family by marrying you."

"But at all events had we not better agree to defer the marriage a little till she gets over her present silly prejudice against me ?"

" Well," answered the other with hesitation ; "perhaps it is weak, but, at your request, I have no objection to yield so far —on the complete understanding that the marriage is only deferred."

" Very well, then : and would it not be as well for you to let her know to-morrow that you are willing to make this concession ?"

" No, it would not," said Jabez in wrath. " What do you take me for, my lord ? I have perhaps been hasty, but at my time of life it is surely too much for any one to expect that I shall ask pardon from a disobedient girl. I am too proud. If she wants grace she must come for it."

"Oh, she'll come, you may depend on it, sooner or later :" Stainmore really believed what he said, for he could not conceive the possibility of any woman throwing away a magnificent fortune from simple dislike to himself, favourite of the sex as he was.

"You really think so ? Well, perhaps she will—she is not a bad girl, after all. And now let us talk about something else —anything but this unpleasant subject."

He walked to the window and threw it open. The night was as wild as ever, the snow thick on the ground and in the air, so that he could only see a few yards, while the wind whirled a quantity of sleet in his face and shook the casement so violently that his utmost strength was required to hold it. He soon slammed it to, therefore, and came back to the fire with a very pale face. After making a great fuss in dashing the particles of snow off his coat, he poured out with an unsteady hand a glass or two of wine, which he drank in quick succession.

"We shall have a great fall of snow before morning, I think—real Christmas weather, Stainmore. Fill your glass again," he said huskily. "My voice is rather hoarse—I must have caught cold with that window. Yes, we shall hear to-morrow of sheep being overblown and all sorts of things."

"Is that a common occurrence here?"

"Very; sometimes a hundred in one flock—but only on the hills, you know; and I never heard of persons being lost about here—you never did, did you?"

"Well, some one was telling me a story one day about a shepherd at Reinsber——"

"Yes, yes, but that was on the moors, you know—a—a very different thing—a thousand feet above this place. And it was years ago. Of course men who are looking after sheep are out all day and are exposed to the weather a much longer time.—But it would be almost impossible, I take it, for travellers to be lost in the valleys now-a-days when the roads are so good?"

"Still I have heard of such instances."

"I think you must be mistaken, my lord," said Jabez sharply. "How did you like Scotland again?"

They tried many subjects but always wandered back in a circle to the old point. At last they went to bed, agreeing that Kate Oliphant would return to her duty in the morning.

CHAPTER VII.

A WALK THROUGH THE SNOW.

WHEN she left the drawing-room, Miss Oliphant ran upstairs for her hat and shawl, which she had thrown off on her return from the village. On coming down again she met Mrs. Hardacre, the housekeeper, who exclaimed in amazement :

" Deary me, Miss Oliphant, you are never going out again, surely—and without a cloak, and in your thin boots? Why mortal man never saw such a night as it is— snow a couple of feet thick, and coming wilder and faster every minute! We shall have fine work with it trampling in to-morrow, I'll warrant. Now do let James fetch you anything you want : do, please ma'am ; don't be so venturesome. He's in the kitchen with the party, but he won't mind being disturbed for you, ma'am."

"Thank you, Mrs. Hardacre, but James will not do. I am going."

"Yes, I see you are going ; going to catch cold, I call it, Miss," replied the housekeeper, with the freedom of an old servant. "Ay, ay ; we shall have nice nursing after this, *I* know. I shall put a quart of my tincture on the simmer for you this very night, if I can find a safe corner among all this upset ; for they come and they go, rush here and rush there, just as if all the house were their own. But let me fetch you your warm cloak—now do, Miss Oliphant—and your thicker boots."

"Well, if you would kindly fetch my cloak—I forgot all about it—but never mind the boots, I had rather not wait for them : these will do."

Mrs. Hardacre fetched the cloak, and put it carefully round her young mistress. "There, that is something like !" she said, when she had finished.

"And would you tie my hat-strings, Mrs. Hardacre ? I have been trying, but my fingers are cold, or something—and this wind will perhaps sweep it off."

"Gracious me, ma'am ! Is something wrong ? You look different, somehow. Surely—surely you are not in trouble ?"

"Thank you ; that will do very nicely. Yes, I am going to leave Reinsber : you will hear all about it, I dare say, before long."

"You—going to leave Reinsber—to-night ?"

"Yes, it is so, indeed. You have all been very good to me, and I should have liked to bid the servants good-bye, but I fear my uncle might not approve—so perhaps you will say it for me, Mrs. Hardacre, —not to-night, for you might interfere a little with their pleasure. And ask them, please, for my sake, to stay with my uncle if they can, and to be very kind and forbearing to him—he will soon be a good deal by himself. I am sorry I cannot quite tell you what has happened ; but—but good-bye, dear Mrs. Hardacre, and thank you very much for all your kindness to me. Mr. Holden has come back, and I am keeping him waiting ; so I must go."

And with a warm shake of the hand she hurried away from the faithful old servant, who stood as if petrified, and evidently only half comprehended what had been said. An instant afterwards Miss Oliphant was in the wild night, and the Hall doors —which she had entered, an hour ago, the heiress of a million, and was leaving a beggar—had closed behind her.

"Well, Kate, I am still lost in amazement at all this. Are *we* awake or dreaming?" asked Holden, as he placed her arm fondly within his own when they plunged into the snow outside: "O darling, what a night for you to be out in!"

"One does not feel it so much when one has more important things to think of," said Kate; adding, with a faint laugh, "I thought the last quarter of an hour you looked as if you had just dropped from the moon, and—what with the shake, what with the new appearance of things in general—were considering the earth a very strange place for a respectable moonist to be in."

"Then you did look at me? that's some comfort."

"Only a second, sir, when I was not better employed; and you seemed as much scared as Lord Stainmore half-an-hour before."

" I confess I was never so much startled in my life. But he will relent; he must relent."

" I do not see the 'must,' and I am sure he never will after what he has said. When he once thinks a thing right he does it, and never changes or regrets it. He will be firm till death, you will see."

" Then it is the most inhuman thing—"

" Nothing of the kind, Frank; and you shall not abuse him. I do not see that he has done anything at all wrong—only something a little bit severe, but just enough from his point of view. I had no right to expect that, because he has been most generous to me for many years, he would continue so always. I was simply a guest, and have out-stayed my welcome, that is all. But I should think myself very base if I lessened my love or respect for him, or my gratitude for what he has done, because he might have done more."

"Still, my dear philosopher, you must own it was abominable to turn you out to-night. Whew! how it drives in our faces!"

"He was angry, and therefore hasty in that, but against this single fit of anger I have to set a thousand kindnesses."

"Then you'll go back to him, and try to talk him over to reason, to-morrow?"

"Nay, Frank, not so. I am as proud as he is. I would have gone to him gladly —for he will be very lonely—if he had not talked about his money. But now—what a curse such fortunes are sometimes!"

"By heaven," said Holden, vehemently, "I could wish I had died in earnest before I caused you to suffer this."

"You cause it, Frank? It was fate. And I am not sorry. Only think: if you had died, I should have married yon man."

"And I should certainly have *walked.*

As an ardent lover and respectable ghost,
I could not have been off it, however warm
or snug the lying might have been in Italy
yonder; he did the best for me he could in
that way, poor man! But imagine—in a
thin winding-sheet, and such weather as
this—hugh!"

"You would have walked too late : it is
a thousand times better as it is," answered
Kate. "How prettily the trees are orna-
mented with snow! Dear Reinsber!"

"Both they and Reinsber will be stripped
of their ornament by morning. Heigh-ho,
so runs the world."

"And I hope gets on faster and easier
than ourselves. Let us imitate this good
sensible world, Frank, and clothe our
thoughts in white instead of black."

"All right ; but, Kate dear, if it is not
an impertinent question, have you any notion where we are going, or what we are

going to do to-night? Bother take the latch—it's as stiff as your uncle. Here we are at the carriage-drive, and I suppose you are not thinking of bivouacking in the snow, like the French on the retreat from Moscow? Come on this side of me, dear; you will be a little more out of the wind."

"Thank you, Frank; I think you *are* the heavier metal, and will be less easily blown away. As for me, I am expecting every minute to be carried up into the air like a balloon."

"They want you in the higher regions, depend on it."

"Seriously, I think of going down to Mrs. Mansfield's and asking her for a bed," said Kate.

"A very good notion. And then?"

"And then—and then, I don't know what then—perhaps trying to get a place as a governess somewhere, or upper ser-

vant; it is generally much the same thing,
I believe. If you hear of anything likely
to suit me, you must let me know. I
can spoil a pudding in the cooking, mis-
pronounce French, and teach a wrong note
as well as most people ; but I won't undertake more than ten children, that's flat."

"I can answer for your having all the
accomplishments. But it is strange : I happen to know the very place for you."

"No, Frank ! But do you really ?" said
Kate, seriously.

"Yes, indeed : and from my intimacy I
can guarantee you the post, if you like to
take it. The head of the family is a genial
sort of fellow, with more heart than brains,
and more brains than money."

" And his wife ?"

" Oh, he is not married at present, and
his hat covers his family. Come, Kate, say
you'll be my governess and director-general

at once. There is no one who will appreciate your services so highly as your humble servant; and if you do not expect a recall from your uncle, and do not mean to go to him again, you are free now to do as you like."

" Ah, Frank, but are you not afraid to make another offer to this splendid heiress of nothing ?"

" By Jove, no !" replied Holden earnestly. " To tell the honest truth, though it may seem rather selfish, I am glad on my own account that you haven't a penny. I think I was mean enough to be rather afraid of you—not much, but still a little bit—when you were a great heiress and I a poor painter. Now that you are nearer me, you shall see what my love is made of. Darling, say yes."

" But how in the world can we live ? We shall starve," answered his companion.

" Then we might as well starve together as starve singly.　Let us try love in a cottage, and show the world that it is possible."

In fine, Holden talked so long to the same effect, that Kate at last agreed to enter into the partnership, and it was fixed that the marriage should take place in London as soon as possible.

From Mr. Oliphant's house to Mrs. Mansfield's at the farther end of the village, the distance was little less than two miles by the nearest route, and rather more by the ordinary carriage-road, which, after leaving the Hall grounds, ran bleak and exposed between bare stone fences the whole way to Reinsber, with scarcely a tree to break the power of the gale that swept directly up the valley in the very teeth of our pedestrians.　The cold sleet therefore drove in their faces, chilling them to the bone, and, as they had literally to force their way through the violent wind, while at each step they sank a foot deep into the soft snow, their progress was so slow and laborious that Frank began to be very much alarmed for Kate.

For the first half mile, indeed, in her excitement she was scarcely aware of any very unusual exertion, though her previous walk to the village had already fatigued her considerably. But when they reached the turnpike road, beyond the partial shelter of the trees in the grounds, every step told on her, and she soon became drowsy and tired. Still she struggled bravely on for a few hundred yards farther, but then she began to reel a little, and several times would have fallen if the artist had not supported her. He encouraged her with his cheery voice, and talked of old times and of everything which he thought would interest her, but she was scarcely conscious, and they were still more than three quarters of a mile from the village when she stopped utterly exhausted.

"Frank, I shall never reach it!" she murmured. "I cannot go another step. You had better hasten on and save yourself if you can."

"Nay, not so, Kate. Rest a minute and try again."

"It is no use. This dreadful wind takes all the life out of me. Well, I did not think of dying thus—but God forgive me if I have done wrong! How sorry my poor uncle will be!" and slipping from the other's arms she fell to the ground.

"You will not die! For my sake, darling!" he cried. "I will carry you. Come!"

"You cannot, dear Frank, as you know; you are not strong yourself."

"Your danger will give me strength."

"But I must sleep a minute—just a minute—and then, perhaps."

"No, no! you must not sleep," he exclaimed. "Sleep is death. For heaven's sake keep awake whilst I carry you!"

"Well, I should not much care if it was the last sleep of all, either," she replied. "But I must sleep a little."

Frank cast his eyes round in despair, and then he shouted again and again, but, except a rather louder swirl of the blast as if in mockery, there was no response, for few persons cared to be out on such a night, and there was not a house or even a barn on the road. It had not escaped Miss Oliphant's notice that the artist was still weak, and in truth the wounds he had received in Italy had shattered his health a good deal. By this time, therefore, he was very much tired himself, and the village seemed to him an infinite distance away still. He scarcely knew what to do. If he left Kate and hurried to procure assistance, he was aware that, even if he reached the houses, he would lose much time on the road, and more in rousing the people, who would be in bed; while the snow was coming down so fast that Kate would be covered and probably dead before they reached her again. Although, therefore, he despaired of accomplishing the distance with such a burden, he perceived clearly that he must trust to himself; so with a silent prayer for strength he whispered to her, "You will not mind my carrying you now, dear?" and raising her in his arms, bore her something like a hundred yards at a very slow pace, when he was forced to put her down and rest. He had observed that without knowing it she had lost one of her boots in the snow, and he occupied his breathing time in tying his handkerchief round her foot.

Kate was in a dreamy state, half awake, half asleep, and she whispered to him with a faint laugh, " We are beginning our gipsy life very soon, dear Frank."

"Yes, dear," he said ; and then trying to rouse her spirits in another way, for he knew that every yard she could walk was of importance : " But this cannot be Kate Oliphant, surely, to give in after this fashion !"

The taunt had its effect, for she rose and staggered on for some distance before she dropped to the ground again.

" I cannot do it. O my poor uncle; I think even he would pity me now !"

He answered with a laugh,—

" I only said it to get you on a bit,—so don't be angry. Now I'll carry you again."

By successive stages he conveyed her within three or four hundred yards of the village, though he only kept her awake by often shaking her without ceremony. But he was now himself completely chilled and exhausted, and he felt a drowsiness stealing over him which he could hardly resist. He leaned panting against the wall by the road-side, first placing Kate's head on his shoulder as he supported her. He thought they might as well die in each other's arms, if they were to die ; and he quite despaired now of reaching the houses, even if Kate were not with him. He gave a last prolonged shout for help, on the very faint hope that somebody in the village might hear him. But no human voice could have been heard more than a few yards against such a wind as was then blowing.

To his surprise, his shout was answered from the other direction. He leaped up, and with redoubled energy called again.

Soon a man in a plaid made his appearance through the obscurity of the driving snow. Holden appealed frantically to him for help.

"Here is Miss Oliphant dying here, if you cannot help us."

"Aa dear, aa dear! Where is she, Mr. Holden?" said the man. "I wor just turning back when I heard you shout, for I thowt you mun hev reached t' village aw reght."

"Why, who are you? You seem to know my name," said the artist.

"Oh, ay. I'se James, t' gardener at t' Haw, an' Mrs. Hardacre sent me efter ye to see ye gat safe to Reinsber. Poor thing! But I niver seed sich a neght. I've been near an hour i' coming this distance mysel. Here's some brandy, I've browt wi' me; give her a drop."

Holden snatched the flask, and gave Kate a little of the spirit. Then he took a draught himself, and his hope of life came back.

“But how was it you did not come before, James, if you came at all?” he asked. “It has been touch and go with us.”

“Why, Mrs. Hardacre nobbut began to be flaid about ye some’at like an hour sin’, when t’ weather didn’t mend : an’ then she teld me, an’ I jumped up an’ left t’ dance an’ iverything.　Bless ye, we’d aw of us do ought for Miss Oliphant.”

“Well, don’t let us lose any more time; we must carry her between us.”

As the fair burden was now divided, they accomplished the remaining distance with comparative ease; but it was nearly eleven o’clock when they reached Mrs. Mansfield’s.　The good old lady was up, and though greatly amazed at this influx of visitors at so late an hour, and in such a plight, gave them a hearty welcome.

James, after a glass of something hot and a handsome present from Frank, started back to the Hall, bearing a strict charge from Kate not to tell anyone, and especially her uncle, of the danger she had been in. When she had hastily swallowed a cup of tea, she also retired to her room, leaving Frank to explain in full the extraordinary events which had led to the visit.

Mrs. Mansfield sat up conversing with him till a late hour about Mr. Oliphant's proceedings, and, as Dora and Mr. Fothergill (who had been made man and wife three months before) were to spend Christmas-day with her, she trusted that her son-in-law's superior acuteness would discover some remedy for what had occurred; while she also stoutly maintained that Jabez, who was often wrong-headed but always meant what was right, would send for Kate in the morning to make matters up.

CHAPTER VIII.

FAREWELL.

NO messenger arrived from the Hall the next morning, and when Mrs. Mansfield expressed her disappointment to Kate, the latter laughed at the notion. She had staid in bed till noon, and was now in good spirits; the only remains of the excitement and exposure of the previous night being a severe cold. By-and-by Fothergill and Dora came in, and the latter flew into Kate's arms, exclaiming,—

" Dear Kate, what shall I say or do to comfort you ?"

Miss Oliphant returned her friend's embrace very warmly, but answered :—

" Well, I think, Dora, your congratulations should come first, should they not?
Our friend Mr. Holden has come back, you
see—unless you mean that we ought to be
consoled for being teased with him once
more."

" I am very, very glad to see dear Mr.
Holden back after such a providential
escape. But I meant—you know what I
meant."

"Of course I do, dear," replied Kate ;
" but you must keep your sympathy for
my uncle, when you see him. It is not
every uncle that can afford to throw off so
admirable and obedient a niece, I can tell
him."

" Miss Oliphant and I have agreed to
make the best of matters, you see, Mrs.
Fothergill," said Holden.

" But it is dreadful to be turned out in
this way without a moment's warning. I
consider it positively wicked of him," re-

turned Dora in tears, and stamping her foot on the ground.

" Now don't use strong language, Dora," said Fothergill, pulling a comical face ; " you know your pretty lectures to me on that text will lose all their effect, if you do. Let us go in to dinner."

Fothergill was unaffectedly glad to see Holden again, and sympathised deeply with Miss Oliphant, though, catching their tone on the subject, he disguised his feelings under pleasantry. The dinner, therefore, was a lively one, and over the dessert —adroitly avoiding, however, any mention of his engagement—Frank once more related his adventures, which all agreed were a famous Christmas story.

Dora now, with a laugh and a blush, whispered something to Frank, who blushed and laughed too, in evident delight. Fothergill observed them, and exclaimed with pretended indignation :

"What, Dora! only three months married, and whispering to another man already! I tell you I'll have no more of this, and if I see Mr. Holden do that again, I shall wish he had staid in Italy. We must have the secret, Dora : speak, I command you : you have promised to obey me, as your sovereign lord, in all things. Out with it !"

"I was only telling him," said Dora, with a sly look at Kate, " that I have never seen Kate so pretty, or so lively, since he was here before."

Kate also coloured and smiled, but turned her face studiously away from Frank.

"O Dora !" she exclaimed, when she had recovered a little from her confusion, but still with her eyes on the table-cloth ; "how can you say so ? Telling tales out of school !"

"Your lord and master graciously forgives your offence, Dora," cried Fothergill, in high glee: "more especially as you've made Kate Oliphant blush for once, which he never could, though he has exposed her various errors and sophistries a thousand times. Hurrah! and so the old engagement is to go on! Mr. and Mrs. Holden, I drink to your health and happiness, with all my heart."

"Well, Kate, there is no use in denying it, is there?" said Holden. "Thank you, Fothergill, most sincerely."

And a round of warm congratulations followed.

"But, William," said Mrs. Mansfield, "I wish to ask you what can be done for our friends here. Surely Kate and Mr. Oliphant cannot be allowed to part in this way."

"Well, I know what I would do if I were Miss Oliphant," replied Fothergill.

"And what is that?"

"Have a writ out *de lunatico inquirendo* against him within a week. There is Hawtrey's affair and now this—-"

"What could make you think of such a thing, Mr. Fothergill?" interrupted Kate, angrily. "My uncle is as much in his sound senses as we are—more than yourself, a good deal, if I were to judge you by your last speech. I think him mistaken in his judgment of Lord Stainmore, and he thinks me mistaken in mine, and we have quarrelled on the subject—nothing more. He is mistaken, too, about Mr. Hawtrey; but to say that he makes mistakes is only to say that he is a man. In my judgment— and I have had better opportunities than yourself of knowing him—he is a very noble and generous man."

"You need not be angry, Kate," answered Fothergill; "I merely said what I should do. As to Stainmore, I certainly think if he had a spark of the gentleman in him, he would have resigned all pretensions to your hand last night, before allowing Mr. Oliphant to go so far. He must have seen very soon that all his own chances were over."

"Nay, poor man," said Kate, "I fancy he did not recover from the sight of Frank in time."

"I often wonder," remarked Dora, with her timid reverent voice striking in like a bit of sacred music, "why God, who is so good and gracious, lets such wicked men live at all. It must be for some good purpose; but why is it, William?"

"Perhaps they are meant," answered Fothergill, smiling kindly at her, "to serve as a foil to such thorough gentlemen as Holden here and myself. If there were only sheep in the world, and no goats, you ladies would be terribly embarrassed how to choose for the best. As it is, you have both been extremely fortunate, and I con-gratulate you with all my heart."

" On having got a couple of sheep, Dora, do you hear ?" said Kate laughingly ; "and oh, the vanity of the two sheep ! But I don't think the couple of them would fetch much in the market—what is mutton a pound, now, Mrs. Mansfield ? We can soon see what they are worth."

"Now that illustrates a failing of the sex, Kate," retorted Fothergill. " You either cannot understand a metaphor, or you push it to death."

The plans of the two lovers were then discussed at length. " There is this good, at any rate, in having no money," cried Frank ; "if there really is anything in a man, poverty will bring it out. It braces the sinews and fires the brain. A rich man may work ; a poor man must : and work his best, too, or he will starve.

Almost all the great things that have ever been done, have been done by poor men."

"I see one who will charge up-hill gallantly, at any rate," said Fothergill. "But look at the other side of the picture—the solitude or society which the rich man may choose as best fits his purpose, the leisure for full contemplation of his schemes, the command of all means and appliances, the time for working out his plan without hurry, mistake, or imperfection. His work ought to be the better of the two when it is finished."

"Which it never will be," said Holden. "Indolence gets on his back, and keeps telling him any hour in the day will do,—he might as well take his time; and he takes his time so well that night comes on when he is miles from his goal. The poor man, on the other hand, is ridden express, and in spurs."

" And so passes by many things that he ought to have noticed," replied Fothergill. " What does my little saint think ?"

" Well, I think the very poor have one great advantage over other people," said Dora; "they know they cannot have treasure upon earth and, as a man would be very unhappy if he had no treasure at all, they naturally look for it elsewhere. So that I think I had rather be very poor than very rich."

" But I would not," remarked Kate; "you will not all of you persuade me into a preference for poverty. I am content to be poor, and will make the best of it; but I should certainly be happier if I were rich : I believe everybody would."

" You will at all events have the opportunity of testing your fashionable friends now," said Fothergill, laughing. " O Kate,

I pity you—have you provided yourself with a wallet small enough ?"

" We do not intend to send the hat round just yet," answered Holden. " We have hands, and mean to work."

" Bravo ! But really, Kate, you had better stay with Dora and me," said Fothergill. " This is too much like a parting dinner to intending emigrants to suit my fancy—some poor wretches that have been turned out of their pleasant cottage by a wrathful landlord, and with eyes and hearts still fixed on the shores they are leaving, are being carried, they do not know where, except that it is to some region peopled with forests and tigers, and as uncouth, and dreary, and horrible, as it is unknown."

" Say, rather," replied Holden, " that we are sailing out bravely with flags flying, exulting hearts, hope at the helm, and the world of waters 'all before us, where to choose.' Like Columbus, we may find a new continent—who knows ? The least I expect is a California."

"Holden, Holden," remarked Fothergill, mournfully, "you have one fault that spoils a good fellow—you live in the future tense."

"And that is better," rejoined Kate, "than sticking all his life at the imperfect, like such a dull boy as yourself, Mr. Fothergill, or brooding sadly and cynically over the past. For myself, the plain, truthful, practical present is the tense for me ; and I should prefer saying that our good ship has met with a storm, no doubt, but has weathered it bravely, and got into a very pleasant harbour, thanks to Mrs. Mansfield here. To-morrow we put out again ; but we are quite seaworthy, and, if another gale comes on, hope to make another port."

"But do stay with us, Kate, as William

asks you," said Dora, with tears in her eyes; "at least till Frank has a good home for you, and can keep you."

"Which may be never, in spite of his California in prospect," answered Kate. "Nay, dear, it is all settled between Frank and myself, and we go to London to-morrow. Naturally, my uncle may not like my staying long in the neighbourhood after what has happened. Till we are married, I shall visit one or two friends in town, who have often pressed me to go and see them. But I thank you very much, all the same; and you too, Mr. Fothergill. I see where I shall begin with my subscription list, when I do start such a thing."

A maid-servant now entered to say there was Dick Wideawake below, who wished to see Miss Oliphant, and "wouldn't be said." The first time he came, she had told him they were at dinner, and now he had called again.

"Pray let him come up, Mrs. Mansfield," said Kate. "I should like very much to see him once more. As Mr. Fothergill says, honest friends are scarce."

"Well, I niver knew ought like this i' aw my born days, Miss Oliphant!" exclaimed the big farmer, as he "came cluntering" into the room, to use one of his own expressions. "Ye aren't *raelly* boun, are ye?"

"Indeed I am, Mr. Wideawake."

"What! an' it's aw true? Then it's a decad loss o' five pund to me sin' church-time. I bet that to Tommy Doolittle off t' stick end 'at there warn't a word o' truth i' aw t' story. He wor fussing about an' telling iverybody—ye knaw his way—an' I warn't boun to hear ye run down, Miss Oliphant. Odd drat it! to be bitten by a lile fool like Tommy! But niver mind, it's nobbut yance, an' I've bit him mony a time. Well, I'se fair capped!"

"Come, sit down, Dick, and let us talk

matters over," said Fothergill. "You are a sharp fellow, and may be able to give us some good advice. Which wine will you have?"

"Don't ye puzzle a chap, Mr. Fothergill; auther on 'em 'll do, if they're good an' plenty on 'em. Here's my respects, Mrs. Mansfield, an' to aw on ye. Mr. Holden, I'se glad to see ye back. Ye found Italy wor even warmer than ye thowt of, I hear. How did ye manish to git out o' t' frying pan into t' fire soa?"

"It was our friend Lord Stainmore's doing, Dick," said Holden.

"I heeard some'at o' t' kind. He's a nasty oily fellow is that, an' there's niver ony good i' too mich greease. I sud just like to come across him efter this wi' a bit o' horse-trading. It 'ud be some satisfaction to yan's conscience, doing *him*, now."

"I am not certain though," said Kate, "that you would keep your laurels if you

exchanged passes with him, Mr. 'Wideawake. He is a very bad but a very clever
man."

"Ay, ay," answered the farmer with a
sly wink, "but I sudn't mind trying. I've
done cuter men nor him afore now, an' it's
all'ays sa mich pleasanter tricking a sharp
fellow than a flat."

"But have you never been tricked yourself, Mr. Wideawake?"

"Eigh—I willn't deny it—twa three
times afore I cut my wisdom teeth, Miss
Oliphant; but niver twice by t' same
man. 'Yance bit, twice shy,' as we say i'
Yorkshire; an' I all'ays manished to tak
full change out on 'em i' t' end, too. Yan
hed to buy yan's experience, of course, an'
yan owtn't to say mich i' yan's own favour,
but sin' I wor twenty, he'd be a bowd man
'at 'ud say he'd mich to brag on i' his deal-
ings wi' Dick Wideawake."

"That he would, you rascal!" cried

Fothergill, smiling. "Do you remember that brown mare you sold me?"

"Oh ay, Mr. Fothergill," answered Dick, putting on his best business face; "she wor an evven-down good un, I knaw. Ye happen don't want another o' t' same mak just now?"

"No, no, indeed I don't, Dick; one of the kind is quite enough. But we will talk about the mare by-and-by. Miss Oliphant is going to leave us to-morrow."

"Ye don't say soa! Nay now, ye willn't do that, Miss Oliphant? Yer uncle hesn't used me weel, but he's a gentleman—I will say that for him; an' it 'ud be varra bad behaviour o' ye if ye left him for a bit of a tiff. Gang tull him—ye're younger o' t' two, Miss Oliphant—an' mak it up, now, like a reght good young lady as ye are."

"So I would with pleasure, my dear Mr. Wideawake," said Kate in tears, "but he has turned me out of the house, and forbidden me ever to go near it again. If I do, he says he shall think I am after his money."

"Well I niver!" said Dick slowly, and scratching his head. "Why, he mun be clean gane daft. Hegh! ye're reght—that's a stockdolocher if he said that. I dunnot see how ye can gang tull him yersel efter that. But, odd dal it, somebody mun!" he added, snatching up his hat and knobbed stick. "It willn't do to let him gang on like this wi' his ain flesh an' blood, an' if ye eren't boun, Mr. Fothergill, I am."

"Goodness gracious! where are you going, Dick?" asked Fothergill in alarm.

"I'se boun to beard t' lion i' his den," answered Dick, sticking his hat energeti·cally on his head and buttoning his coat as if in preparation for a fight. "I'se boun to Reinsber Haw, to be sure. Ye're t' man to do it, an' ye'd better come wi' me, if ye ern't flaid. What, man! we munnot let a lile fatherless thing be trampled on i' this fashion, acos he's sa rich an' she hes naebody to stand up for her. I couldn't sleep if we did ; an' that 'ud be a fearful thing for me—folk wi' mich flesh want a deal o' sleep. Now, are ye coming, Mr. Fothergill ?"

I believe myself that the honest farmer with his vigorous sallies might just possibly have stormed Mr. Oliphant's entrench- ments, weakened as they were no doubt by his night's sleep. But the rest of the party would not let Dick go, fearing that Jabez might be still more exasperated against Kate by such an intrusion. Miss Oliphant, though grateful to the farmer for a proposed interference which in the case of her uncle required no little courage, joined her entreaties to those of the others ; and at last Dick sat down again, gloomy and grumbling.

"Nay then, if ye're again' me too, Miss Oliphant, I willn't," he said. "Ye 'at are scholards owt to knaw better nor me, but I think mine's t' best plan efter aw; an' if I come across him, begow, I sall let fly."

"But not till I am gone, please, Mr. Wideawake," said Kate.

"Well, then, I'll promise ye that. Aa, Miss Oliphant, but Reinsber 'll be a different place when ye've left it. I cannot tell ye how sorry I is. Ye're boun to Lunnon, then?"

"Yes."

"Well, ye willn't find as pretty or as good a lass there as yersel, that's aw. But I'll tell ye what: Lunnon's a sad smoky hoil, I've all'ays heard; an' when ye want a bit o' raal fresh country air, just ye come down to Sandy Topping an' stay as lang as iver ye like—t' langer t' better. I knaw we ern't gentlefolk like ye, but t' wife and I 'll try to mak ye comfortable. Ye'll hev t' best parlour an' t' best bed-room an' t' best of iverything : t' wife's rayther house-proud,

an' iverything's varra clean, if it's plain :
an' if ye're a bit sick or owt o' that, there
isn't sich cream, or eggs, or butter ony-
where i' England as there is at t' Topping,
though I say it.   Now I'se expect ye, Miss
Oliphant."

Kate thanked him most cordially and,
when he rose to go, Fothergill shook his
hand warmly, and said, " You're a right
good fellow, Dick, and I shall not say
another word about that brown mare."

Dick grinned, but though he had bid
them good-bye, he was a long time in finding first his hat and then his stick, and
afterwards shuffled rather uneasily about
the room, as if he wished to say something
more ; but he finally vanished, and they
heard his heavy foot descending the steps
very slowly.   When he got to the bottom
of the staircase, however, his deep, jolly
voice came rumbling up to them again ; he
was evidently trying hard to reduce it to

what he considered the tones of polite-
ness :—

" Hist! hi! Miss Oliphant!" he shouted;
then he ejaculated to himself, " Dal it, I
mak as mich noise as t' town clock even
when I want to talk soft."

Kate made her appearance at the top of
the stairs.

"I say, Miss Oliphant, I just want
another word wi' ye, by yersel, if ye please,"
said Dick, sheepishly.

" I'll come down, then, Mr. Wideawake.
There, now we can talk quite privately."

" Well, ye'll excuse me, but I didn't like
to say it afore 'em aw. I'se flaid, frae what
I heard, ye'll be badly off for brass; if I'se
mistakken, ye mun forgive me : now, I've
three or four hundred pound i' Stainton
Bank 'at I don't want mich wi'. Just let
me send it to ye on t' sly, now; naebody
sall knaw but wer two sels, and ye knaw
Lunnon's a varra expensive an' a varra

dangerous place : ye've all'ays bin used to live like a lady, an' ye'll want money there."

" O Mr. Wideawake !" was all Kate could say, for she was deeply affected at this new token of the honest farmer's generosity.

"Ye knaw ye can pay me back if iver ye're rich again, an' if ye aren't I salln't grudge it. I'se weel to do, ye knaw, an' horse-jobbing's a rare business—to them 'at understands it, of course. Sae we sall niver miss t' brass at aw."

" Nay, nay—there are your children."

" Oh, t' childer mun feght their way, like their daddy afore 'em. It'll do 'em nae harm to wark—they're used to it; but ye —Lord bless us ! Come, now, say ye'll tak it wi'out mair ado, an' I'se gang hame satisfied, Miss Oliphant. I isn't easy about yer ganging i' this way."

" Indeed, indeed, Mr. Wideawake, I could not take your hard-earned money;

but I feel how generous you are, and I am deeply grateful for all your kindness. I— I ought to tell you—" here Kate blushed very prettily amid her tears, "but you must not tell anybody except Mrs. Wideawake just yet, please: I am going to be married directly to Mr. Holden, and, though we shall be very poor, we hope to get on well."

"I'se glad to hear it, Miss Oliphant," said the horsedealer, "an' I wish ye joy wi' aw my heart. He's a reght down honest chap, is Mr. Holden; it all'ays struck me he wor Yorkshire bred, he hes sich a happy face: but I niver liked to ax him. But are ye sure ye willn't want t' brass? Hev some on it—ye'll find ye've a deal to pay, furnishing and house-keeping. Bless ye, I sudn't wonder butter 'll be fifteen pence a pund i' Lun-non, an' other things i' like manner."

"Thank you, we must not begin borrowing already. But if ever we really cannot get on at all, I will apply to you the very first."

Dick's face brightened at this assurance : " I suppose I mun be content wi' that ; but I'se expect ye to keep yer promise, Miss Oliphant. If iver ye want money, ye'll let me knaw : it's an understood thing now, isn't it ?"

He was then bidding her good-bye, when Kate suddenly exclaimed, " Nay, dear Mr. Wideawake, if you will adopt me as your daughter, you must not let us part like this ;" and, putting a hand on his shoulder, she offered her blushing cheek to his salute.

" Aa, *wadn't* aw t' handsome young chaps i' Stainton think me a lucky fellow, Miss Oliphant, if they knew ? Ye'd hev 'em aw offering their bit o' brass," whispered Dick with a sly smile, as he vanished through the door.

Kate had several other visits that afternoon from her poor friends in the village, who came in wonder and trepidation to bid her good-bye.   Towards night, Mrs. Hardacre brought her a note from the Hall to the following effect :—

"*Private.*

"DEAR MISS OLIPHANT,—

" Although I am so unfortunate as to have incurred your severe displeasure, I trust you will excuse my writing to inform you that I have, with great difficulty, and on condition that you will come and see him, prevailed on your uncle to *defer* the marriage on which he is still so much bent. It seems to me, therefore, you would only be acting wisely in temporizing, by giving him your promise to marry, as he wishes, *at some indefinite future time*—of course with the perfect understanding between ourselves that such promise is merely given to make your peace with him.   I need not

say that if I find you, after full considera-
tion, and when you no longer allow your
anger to sway your judgment, still disposed
to think so unjustly of my poor innocent
self, I shall of course consider myself in
honour bound to withdraw from our engagement.

"Your humble and very unhappy servant,

"STAINMORE.

"P.S.—In your interview with Mr. Oliphant, it would be only prudent to make
some slight apology, and please do not say
that you have heard from me."

Kate's first impulse was to tear the note
into shreds and send no answer; but she
restrained her indignation so far as to dash
off the following reply :—

"MY LORD,—

"Your note is like yourself. After trying to assassinate Mr. Holden and deceiving

me, you wish me to deceive my uncle with
a promise which I would die sooner than
fulfil. The road of duplicity may be dreary
enough with an evil conscience and bad
dreams, but you shall not beguile it by
having for your fellow-traveller

" KATE OLIPHANT."

The rest of the evening was spent in chat
and needful preparations for the journey to
London in the morning.

CHAPTER IX.

MORE OLIPHANTIASIS.

LORD STAINMORE did not remain long at the Hall after the explosion. In two or three days he came to the conclusion, both from Kate's flight to London, and still more from her note to himself, that a reconciliation between uncle and niece was an impossibility at present; and this being the case, he very soon grew tired of Mr. Oliphant's conversation, which just now was even less lively than usual.

Mrs. Oliphant, too, had departed on Christmas-day, for she found Jabez quite as resolute in the morning as he had been the night before. In truth her failings and his own lay in such opposite directions, that he was secretly glad to find an opportunity for getting quit of her. But as he granted her an annuity of three hundred a year, even she allowed that " he behaved very handsomely."

Mr. Oliphant, therefore, was left alone in the great house. He did not like his solitude ; nay, he felt it bitterly : for as he had never been a very social man, and was generally brooding by himself over his projects for world-driving, Kate's voice had been for years the only thing that stirred his feelings and affections very deeply. Perhaps, too, just as we appreciate the nightingale more highly on account of its singing when other birds are asleep, he liked *his* music all the better from his having no other—I cannot say. But, however much he felt the separation, he wrapped himself up in his pride—at first, with a weak fond hope that she might still return to ask for pardon, and then, as the days went by and she made no sign, with a gradual hardening of his heart against her. He began to think himself a very ill-used man. "She might treat," he argued, "even if she is not prepared to submit; she cannot expect a proud old man to make the first overtures, and I will not. She uses me as she would use a stranger—as a stranger, then, let her be!" He quite forgot—one is so apt in one's quarrels to forget such things—that in his anger he had thrown out insinuations which effectually barred the return of any girl, except a mean-spirited fortune-hunter.

It was characteristic of the man that, almost day by day, he dictated to himself in exact words the terms on which he would receive her back: at first they were not very hard, but, as time went on, they became harsher and harsher whenever he polished up in his mind the expressions he intended to use. Soon after the quarrel, he forbade her name to be mentioned in his hearing; and he now tried his best, though it was more difficult, to forget, or at least to hate, her. But of these inward struggles no one who saw him was conscious. People only observed that every week he grew prouder and more reserved, as well as more determined than ever to carry things with a high hand.

For some time, then, his thoughts ran almost entirely on his niece; but as he became accustomed to his solitude, they gradually returned into their old channel. If he had not much private happiness, he must, at any rate, now as ever, live for the public good; and the public good demanded in his opinion the sacrifice of no less a personage than Sir George Highside, whose late behaviour he had not forgotten. Constantly on the watch, therefore, for an opportunity, he contrived, before long, to punish him.

The baronet was fond of a good dinner, and seldom retired from one without a greater quantity of port about him than he could carry at all steadily. One day towards the end of January, he had been dining early with Mr. Carlton, and was returning home about seven. He was walking as far as the Red Lion, where he had left his horse, and was waddling along in the clear moonlight with a pretentiously solemn gait, taking the wall of the passers-by, as he invariably did, even when tipsy, from a latent consciousness of the dignity at all times appertaining to a Highside.

This unlucky night, however, he had nearly

reached the centre of the village, when, after successfully rounding a very difficult corner, he suddenly met Mr. Oliphant, who was advancing loftily with slow and majestic strides in the opposite direction. If you can picture to yourself the meeting at sea of a heavy, rolling, badly-built and badly-steered Dutch lugger, a clumsy and lumbering tub, with a tall and stately yacht, well in hand, and the pride of some nobleman's heart, you have something like the appearance of the two men at the instant. I do not say, like his enemies, that Jabez had sought for this meeting on purpose; though I think he was not ill-pleased at it, and had taken no special pains to avoid it. Sir George and he had 'cut' one another completely since the dinner at Reinsber Hall, and the baronet was a good deal more inclined to stand on his dignity with him than with any one else.

"Do you not yet know your proper side of the footpath, sir?" said Jabez, haughtily coming to a stand as the baronet was taking the wall of him.

Sir George, conscious of being in the wrong, did not contest the point farther, though his indignation rose to overflowing. With an indistinct muttering of "Cobbler's son—giving himself airs as usual!" he tried to step aside and so pass Mr. Oliphant. Dutch luggers, however, that are badly steered, should not venture too near other ships, and the sudden change of direction proved fatal to the baronet's equilibrium; for, in passing, he miscalculated by a few inches the required distance and, without in the least intending to do so, reeled against Jabez so as to graze his left shoulder slightly.

"This is either an assault, sir," said Mr. Oliphant, "or you are too drunk to be able to guide yourself. In either case your conduct is disgraceful. Did you intend to push me, sir ?"

"Yes, sir,—d—e, yes—if you like. Who are you, taking wall of your betters ?" retorted the angry baronet with much more to the same effect.

" Thomas, will you fetch Mr. Doolittle ?" said Jabez to his footman, whom he had brought with him to carry a parcel.

Tommy Doolittle lived close by, and, at the summons of his patron, was on the spot in a moment, with his staff of office. The footman had not told him who it was that Mr. Oliphant was in dispute with.

"Mr. Doolittle," said Jabez coolly, " I give this person into your care on a charge of assaulting me, and for being drunk and disorderly in the streets. I request you to take him into custody."

Frank Holden would have enjoyed sketching the faces of the group, just after this speech—the sniggering footman in the background, Tommy Doolittle white and fairly trembling with horror, the plump baronet with his feathers up in rage and astonishment, and Mr. Oliphant towering above with features unmoved and inexorable, a very statue of implacable justice. Sir George recovered his tongue first.

" Me, sir,—arrest me ?" he screamed. "Impudent scoundrel !—mushroom !—I am Sir George Highside of Highside Castle, sir,—old family, not a mushroom. Arrest me! You dare not—much as your life's worth. I am a magistrate, sir."

"You are not a credit to the bench at any rate, sir. Why do you not take him, Mr. Doolittle ?" said Jabez.

" Oh, sir,—oh, please don't, Mr. Oliphant," ejaculated the frightened grocer: "It is Sir George, sir,—you can't have seen him right, I think, sir,—it is night and perhaps rather dark, sir."

"Dark, Mr. Doolittle!" answered Jabez; "why, the moon makes it as bright as mid-day. Of course it is Sir George Highside, but what difference does that make? If I had desired you to take a working man into custody under such circumstances, I presume you would do it?"

"Yes, sir; yes, sir; anything of that kind."

"Well, then, here is a man of position rioting about the streets, and I beg to inform you that the law of England makes no distinction between him and the poor man. I who give him into custody am answerable if the charge is unjust, not you. Take him up without more ado."

"Take me if you dare, Doolittle," spluttered the baronet; "I'll knock your head off, if you touch me."

" You see for yourself," remarked Jabez, " how unreasonably violent he is and how incapable of taking care of himself—in his present state : he ventures even to resist the officers of justice. Will you do your duty ?"

Now, Mr. Oliphant got all his groceries at Doolittle's shop and Sir George none ; so at last the much-perplexed constable advanced his hand, but as cautiously as if he were going to touch fire : " I'm afraid I must do it, Sir George," he said in a quaking voice : " I can't help myself : I—I take you in charge."

The baronet shook off the hand that just touched his shoulder, and, quavering about in frantic indignation, began to show fight and abuse them both still more vehemently.

" He resists you ? Very well ; it only increases his offence," said Jabez philosophically. "As a magistrate, he ought to know better, and of course he will hear of all this to-morrow. But perhaps, as we have his name, and he seems to have such a violent dislike to your taking him into custody like any other person, it will be enough if you see him safely out of the village,—taking care that he makes no further disturbance." And Mr. Oliphant turned on his heel and walked off, leaving the baronet still discharging his rage at him.

Tommy Doolittle took care to construe Mr. Oliphant's last injunction very freely and contented himself with watching from a safe distance the baronet's unequal progress towards the Lion. Sir George had just mounted his horse and was trotting off as Mr. Oliphant returned after doing his business in the village.

"Sir George is very tipsy," he remarked

to the ostler who was watching from the inn-door the baronet's departure.

" Ay, but t' horse 'll manish to keep under him ; it all'ays does, Mr. Oliphant," replied the man with a laugh.

Jabez had now got an arch-rebel on the hip, and was by no means disposed to forego his advantage. Next day, therefore, he summoned the baronet for being drunk and disorderly, and also for assault. To any one who ventured to remonstrate, on the ground of the baronet's age and position, the slightness of the offence, or the ill-will that would follow, Jabez had a dozen ingenious answers, without having occasion to allude even once to the grand reasons which influenced him, namely, Sir George's support of Hawtrey, and opprobrious expressions to himself. These reasons, in fact, he kept carefully out of sight, regarding them perhaps as a sort of reserve force of which it would not be well to let the enemy know the existence.

But he told the objectors (to whom he was always courteous if they staid to hear his reasoning in full, but most of them chanced to be in a great hurry), that far from mitigating his fault, Sir George's age and position aggravated its enormity ; his years ought to have given him experience, his magisterial functions to have taught him the law, and his birth decorum. Nor did Jabez consider the offence a slight one ; for drunkenness was the cause of half the crime in England, and to resist even in an infinitesimal degree the Functionary of Justice, which Thomas Doolittle then was, was to strike at the very root of all law. As to any odium he might himself incur in doing what he thought right, he despised it—as he had often had occasion to despise it before. He esteemed it one of the highest duties of an influential personage (and it was a duty which could only be performed by such), to show all men sometimes that there was one law both for rich and poor, and that as justice found none too low to notice, so she knew none too high to strike down. The aristocracy of England were by no means in as satisfactory a state as he could wish, and if they would not set the example they ought, an example must be made of them.

In fine, William Fothergill, who was one of the objectors, went away overwhelmed, and told Dora he verily believed Mr. Oliphant was contemplating the establishment of Missions to Belgravia. William said " he quite agreed with Jabez so far as this, that the district so named was the most utterly neglected under the sun ; for while hypocrisy, debauchery, and infidelity were rampant there, he could not hear that even an attempt had ever been made to grapple with the evil. It was as much a *terra incognita* to our missionaries as the region about the North Pole, and he believed it was a fact that not one single religious or charitable society existed in it for the benefit of the residents—the upper ten thousand, as they called themselves.

"A gigantic remedial effort, however, he was happy to say, would very shortly be made. The London and Westminster was to be turned immediately into a penny bank; and, for the purpose of attracting the benighted inhabitants to some kind of religious worship, full-dress churches had been thought of. To prevent light conversation, scripture-readers would be engaged to attend at the various drawing-rooms, and there were to be proper clothing-clubs, and midnight meetings for peeresses who did not get on well with their husbands or got on too well with other ladies' husbands. Buildings, too, after the model of Mechanics' Institutes, would be provided, where all persons above a certain rank might spend an innocent evening in listening to instructive lectures ; but cards, billiards, and smoking were to be prohibited there, and the greatest care would be taken to prevent excess in the refreshments allowed, which were to be tea and coffee only.

" Mr. Spurgeon had kindly volunteered to devote a night or two to instructing the editor of the *Saturday Review* in the first elements of Christian charity, making them of course as amusing as possible ; while the editor of the *Record*, with all his staff and all the talent and learning of the great Literate body, had undertaken after some hesitation to wait *en masse* on Mr. Gladstone, and attempt his conversion offhand. This was the only case in which any failure was anticipated, for, as the editor (he believed) had expressed it, 'Mr. Gladstone was a very devil for argument.' Mr. Oliphant had also engaged an able national schoolmaster and two or three forward Sunday-school teachers to read a paper on the Bible before Sir Charles Lyell, Professor Huxley, and other men of science—the paper to be copiously illustrated with extracts, but no discussion to be permitted after it.

"No doubt the first outlay would be very large; but, as such a society had now become a necessity, it was hoped that the masses would take up the scheme and do something for a class which had done so much for them."

Fothergill parodied Mr. Oliphant's usual style so well that for a little bit Dora really thought Jabez had been arranging some plan of the kind mentioned. When her husband had done, however, she laughed and exclaimed :

" O William, and so it is all a romance ! He has no notion of the kind, surely ?"

" Well, he is determined to fine Sir George, as a first step,—that is all I can say ; for you see I am quite out of breath with talking so much."

" Time for you to be out of breath when you talk such nonsense. Poor Sir George ! I am very sorry for him—such a disgrace ! But pray, did Mr. Oliphant say anything about Kate ?"

" Nay, but I said something about her, and you should just have seen him, Dora ! By Jove, I had to pick my way out of the subject as gingerly as if I had been in a powder - magazine with a lighted candle."

But to resume. Mr. Oliphant not only brought his case before the magistrates but won it. He got two or three newspaper reporters down, and employed a very able lawyer, who summoned Thomas the footman, Thomas the constable, the ostler from the Red Lion, and Jabez himself as witnesses, and who bullied the justices whenever they showed the least signs of grace to the distinguished culprit. The latter very wisely did not put in an appearance, and his lawyer contented himself with trying to make the witnesses for the prosecution contradict themselves. Right loth were their worships to find the case proved, for Sir George was considered a great star among them and had often sat on that very bench as chairman; but after two or three hours' deliberation, having a wholesome dread of Mr. Oliphant's sharp lawyer and the newspapers, they felt themselves under the necessity of fining the baronet ten shillings and costs ; and Jabez left the courthouse in triumph : he had not been so happy for many a day.

Encouraged by his victory he called a week or two afterwards on Mr. Truman. It was noon, but Joseph was still in his slippers and was busy writing his next Sunday's discourse, with a litter of papers, dusty theological books, fishing tackle and packages of flower-seeds spread on the table of his dingy parlour. Wiser men try to conceal their poverty, but Truman rather paraded his than otherwise.

" May I ask," said Jabez, after some conversation on general topics, " if you have at all changed your mind about the excommunication of Mr. Hawtrey ? Or have my arguments not yet produced the impression I expected ?"

" I am sorry, as I said before," replied Truman with firmness, " that I cannot do it. My conscience would not allow me."

" For the reasons you alleged in our previous interview ?"

" Yes ; because I cannot believe that my friend Hawtrey, whom I have known ever since I was a lad, has done anything wrong ; and because, if I believed it ever so much, I could not honestly act without having downright proof of his criminality."

" Well, I am the last person to interfere between you and your conscience, for it is a great thing to find any one who has a conscience at all, and I respect such a man. So I will not press you further in this matter."

Mr. Oliphant emphasized the ' this,' and the parson exclaimed in dismay, " Why, surely, you don't mean, Mr. Oliphant, that there's anything else of the same kind which you want me to do— another excommunication, eh ? Goodness gracious, I might be the pope instead of a

poor country parson. I can’t do it—I can’t
do it, I tell you. You are too bad—you
take one so by surprise.”

“ You quite misapprehend me, Mr. Truman,” replied Jabez, smiling at what he
considered an unintentional compliment to
his address ; “but you were right in sup-
posing that I wish you to do something else at
my request—as a favour to myself—though
I do not often ask favours. But it is a mere
trifle—a thing which I am quite sure your
own sense of what is right would have
pointed out to you soon, even without my
hinting it to you. You will do it at once,
I am certain.”

“ Well, what is it ?” asked Joseph in a
doubtful tone : “ My obligations to you
are very great, Mr. Oliphant, as you well
know, and I’ll do it gladly if I can do it
con-sci-en-tious-ly.”

“ Your conscience will be tender indeed

to start at this. You have heard, of course, that Sir George Highside has been very properly fined for gross drunkenness and disorderly conduct?"

"Lord bless us, Sir George Highside! I won't, Mr. Oliphant — I won't. You might as well ask me to excommunicate the whole parish — you might indeed, now."

"I do not wish you to excommunicate him, if you will only have a moment's patience. I simply asked if you had heard of the circumstance I mentioned."

"Ya-as, I did hear something about your having fined him."

"And you are aware, no doubt, that this failing is—has been *proved*, Mr. Truman, in open court to be—habitual. You may have observed his tendency to dissipation yourself, but we will now speak only of what is absolutely proved."

"Well?" said the incumbent, impatiently.

"Now, I know that you have been accustomed to visit him frequently—I have no doubt you were as welcome a guest there as at other places, my dear sir,—in fact, I hear that you drank tea at the Castle only last night."

"Yes, I did. I am fond of a chat, and I have a habit of dropping in to see all my acquaintances now and then in a friendly way, taking any meal with them that is going—just as I do with you at the Hall. No harm in that, I hope?"

"Certainly not, generally. On the contrary, it is a very kind act. But with regard to Sir George Highside, now that these habits have been openly proved against him, I put it to you as a Christian and a clergyman, if it would not be better to give up these friendly visits to him, at any rate till he signifies his determination to reform. The case is so simple that I am sure a moment's reflection will make you agree with me."

"I really don't see why I should give up these visits," answered the parson, completely brought to bay at last.

"The 'why' is very plain, Mr. Truman. If you visit him now you will be countenancing vice."

"Countenancing vice! You might as well say I am countenancing the presence of pike in the river because I go to the river bank to catch trout."

"Your illustration is not very appropriate, and if it were, it is no argument. Here is a notorious drunkard, and yet you, a clergyman, will visit him as if nothing were amiss!"

"One infinitely greater than myself visited the publicans and sinners, Mr. Oliphant," said Joseph reverently.

" Yes, to reform not to jest with them," retorted Jabez.

" But that He might reform, He first showed them friendship and sympathy, by sitting at meat with them. If the baronet were the greatest possible scoundrel, I might still do him a little good by going to see him sometimes ; I can do none if I stay away altogether. I am not a mesmerist—I cannot influence persons who are not in the same room with me."

" What will your congregation think of you, sir ?"

" I really can't help it," replied the parson in desperation, " if either you or they choose to think erroneously of me. But you must pardon me if I consider Sir George up to the average of men, though he has his failings."

" Which you think you can correct over the genial dinner table ! Ah, well ; I confess I am very much disappointed, Mr. Truman. Your notions of a clergyman's duty seem very strange.—May I ask what they are, as they appear so different from my own ?" he added sharply.

" I can answer for no clergyman but myself, Mr. Oliphant," replied the incumbent. " I was never ambitious of becoming an oak when nature meant me for a cabbage; so considering it in very good hands, I have long since given up all care about the world at large."

" Then, yourself ?"

" Well, I neither think myself better nor worse than other men because I wear a surplice ; and my notion of my duty is to live in charity with all my parishioners, pray for them when well, and visit them when sick ; to make my sermons short, sincere, and homely ; to be always ready for my Master's call, and, when the day's trudge is over, to lie down hopefully among my flock, with no wish for a grander epitaph than that of 'an honest Christian.'"

"This is all very well as far as it goes," returned Jabez; "but I can give my support to no minister of the gospel who will not strike a blow with me against vice in high places."

"I cannot satisfy myself that what you propose would do any good, and therefore I cannot help you."

"You might try my plan."

"And mortally offend one of the most influential of my parishioners!"

"Well, you must choose between him and me. To my mind it is the old question between vice and virtue again."

"I am quite firm," said Truman, meekly.

"Then I am very sorry, Mr. Truman," answered Jabez, in decided but courteous tones; " but you have your idea and I have mine as to the proper conduct of a clergyman in such a crisis as this, and unfortunately those ideas are so widely apart that I do not see how they admit of any further intercourse between us. Nor, when in my humble opinion you have such mistaken and imperfect notions of your duty, do I even feel justified in continuing the increase of stipend which I have hitherto given you. If you alter your determination, I shall be glad to see you at the Hall as usual."

The tears stood in the poor parson's eyes as he was thus summarily 'cut' and reduced for conscience-sake from what he considered affluence to his old miserable pittance of seventy-two pounds odd. Still he shook hands with Jabez very charitably; and the latter went home somewhat sorry, but not seeing how, in the interests of this virtue which required so much looking after, he could possibly himself have acted otherwise.

CHAPTER X.

LOVE IN A COTTAGE.

KATE and Frank were married about six weeks after Christmas Day. It was a very quiet wedding, taking place on a very dull day and at one of the dullest of the forlorn London churches, with a deaf old rector as officiating clergyman, and without display of any kind. The bride was given away by a distant relative with whom she had been staying in London ; and there was not a soul in the church except this gentleman, the parson and clerk, the groom's-man and bridesmaid, and of course the happy pair themselves. I am sorry I cannot even describe the bride's dress for the benefit of any young ladies who may grace my pages by glancing over them ; but even if the material had been recorded, which I do not find to be the case, I fear the 'get-up' was so studiously plain and, in spite of its exquisite neatness, looked so very like an every-day dress, that Miss Oliphant's taste might scarcely have risen in their estimation. I can only plead in reply that her face and figure were so perfect that she looked well in anything ; and that Frank, who after all was the chief person concerned, was completely satisfied.

In truth Kate in her altered circumstances was well aware of the absolute necessity of strict economy, if she and her husband were to exist at all, and was sensible enough to know that it was better to begin saving at once. By nature she was fond of having all things about her as fashionable and elegant as possible, without the slightest regard to cost ; and, had she been married like herself from Reinsber Hall, I have no doubt there would have been at least eight or ten pretty brides-maids to wait on her, with such an array of silks, satins and lace, such avenues of glowing flowers from a dozen London green-houses, such a procession of carriages, and such a fashionable assemblage at the grand wed-ding-breakfast, as would have amazed Reinsber for several weeks with the dis-play. There would have been, I will venture to say, a bishop to perform the ceremony and a peeress or two to compliment her after it; and, what she would have liked still better, there would have been all the little girls in Reinsber to scatter flowers before her, and feasting, shouting and jubilee among young and old. And she would have enjoyed all this as much as any one. Now, however, she was very severe on the question of expense and kept a strict rein on Frank, who, though he disliked fuss generally, was disposed to be most extravagant on the present occasion.

After such a wedding, then, and a short trip to the Isle of Wight, Mr. and Mrs. Holden returned to town. With some hesitation, Kate wrote her uncle a brief letter informing him of her change of name. In the note she said she felt that the intimation was due to him after all his kindness to her, though she feared he might misconstrue her intention in writing, and might even be angry with her for venturing to address him. With this exception she did not touch at all on the recent quarrel, but every sentence was full of deep affection. As she expected, Mr. Oliphant took not the slightest notice of her letter.

Their only income was from Frank's labours at the easel, and this, as he was little known in London, was extremely small and precarious. Hence, although they were content with very humble lodgings, there was plenty of pinching. Kate used laughingly to declare that, after the most diligent research, she had utterly failed to discover that London shop which Mr. Wideawake spoke of, where fresh butter was only fifteen pence a pound. She had tried reason, laughter, and remonstrance, each in turn, on the inexorable dairy-men, but could not reduce the price an iota under one and six. She had built somewhat, she averred, on this statement of Mr. Wideawake's, as she had a high opinion of his veracity; but if she had known fresh butter was one and six, instead of fifteen pence, well—it might have gone any way, she was not quite sure she would have been married at all.　She rather thought Frank must have cajoled Mr. Wideawake somehow into this atrocious mis-statement, for the purpose of securing herself and her enormous fortune : and she would write to the good farmer for an explanation, only that he would be sure to send her back a fifty-pound note or something of the kind.　Then there was mutton !　One might think, from its price, the sheep had walked all the way from Kamschatka and lodged at the most expensive hotels on the road too; and as for the beef, she expressed a decided opinion that the London cows could only be fattened on diamonds or gold dust—some peculiarity in the air, she thought, but it certainly made steaks very dear.

Still our friends were always in excellent spirits and wonderfully happy.　Frank toiled very hard, rising at six to get a couple of hours before breakfast ; he then worked on again till one, when they dined, as poor people should. In the afternoon they walked in the streets or parks. In the evening Frank set to work again for five or six hours, either sketching or doing something which did not require daylight, while Kate sang or read to him. But he was never so busy as not to be able, without interrupting his work, to throw out a sly joke or two at Kate, when she sat by the fireside sewing or listening to the music of the domestic kettle. His wife, however, generally paid him back with interest.

One of his favourite amusements on these occasions was to build those cheap and splendid edifices, called castles in the air, which Kate on the other hand was rather fond of demolishing. With Frank it was generally, " When I have the pleasure of introducing you, Kate, to my more luxurious mansion in St.

James's Square, to which the very handsome apartments you see here are merely, I
assure you, the entrance-hall ;" or, " When
my picture gets into the Academy and the
Times ;" or, " When I have finished my
chef d'œuvre, yet to be begun, but which will
secure for us both a glorious immortality."

Kate at these times would ask him
if he knew that butcher's meat had
risen a farthing a pound ; or if he could
possibly let her have a little more pin-
money : or she expressed her apprehension
that the settlements on herself would not
hold good when he came to such a fortune
in the air ; or declared slily that she had
no present intention of leaving these rooms
where they were so comfortable.   Not but
that she sympathized (as only a true wife
can, and as Frank knew) with all his aspi-
rations, and was proud of him also.   If the
jokes were small, at least they drove away

care, and our young couple were easily pleased; for their hearts were light and hopeful, and were beating in unison and love.

Thus the Holdens vanish from our tiny rustic stage; and thus it came to pass, that in one snug nook at any rate even of that great dingy city, with its endless noise and bustle and smoke and misery, many a pretty little pastoral, as sweet as those fabled by Theocritus, was really said or acted. Thank heaven, we may hope that in England there are tens of thousands of families, which, if they have to struggle hard to keep the wolf from the door, do it, like Frank and Kate Holden, with good humour, and make the best of everything.

CHAPTER XI.

A CONSPIRACY, AND THE FALL OF MR. OLIPHANT.

THE term of Mr. Oliphant's power was now near an end. So many persons about Reinsber had felt the weight of his arm, that a powerful coalition was at last formed against him with the object of meting out to him something of the measure he had given others.

The sagacious and powerful mind of Fothergill, delighting in stratagem—if we may here follow the Homeric vein of the original MSS., in describing an event so untoward to our king of men—was that which first conceived a plot so dire. To

him were added the mild wisdom of Hawtrey, lord of the ferule, and the ponderous
strength of Wideawake ferocious in conflict,
among Craven dalesmen chief. From distant homes came they both to attend the
spirit-reviving council, that from the birch-
resounding halls of Stainton, this from
Sandy Topping, fertile in rocks and heather.
Thither too, breathing battle, eager for the
fray, came the Highsides, father and son,
both the horse-loving Harry and Sir George,
the fiery-faced ; no six men could drink the
quantity of twenty-port which (at least*) he
did, daily consuming it alone,—such men
as now live. Nor was loud-voiced Truman
absent, though in his heart he loved not
war or murderous battle ; nor' yet Carlton
good at beeves. All these and more were
gathered in the smoke-rejoicing parlour of

* There is an awkward γε here, of which the editor
can make nothing.

the Red Lion till the little room was full of them, to see if haply for the sons of mortal men deliverance might yet be found from the unappeasable wrath of Jabez. Even as when—but thank you, I think that will do, my dear prince of poets, as we seem to be coming to a six-line simile about a lion and hunters.

The conspirators met, then, at the Red Lion; and Sir George, having been voted into the chair *nem. con.*, called on Fothergill to state the object of the meeting. William was about to comply when Dick Wideawake, who had been asked to attend with Hawthornthwaite to represent the farmers and working men, brought down his clenched fist on the deal table with some force.

"Dal it, Sir George," he exclaimed, " wi' aw respect, ye mun be forgitting yersel awtogither. We owt to order what we want, first, I say. It's like trying to git butter out o' churn milk, is takking counsel wi'out a glass afore yan. What, a single noggin 'll harm nane on us; an' talk dry-lipped I nauther can nor will."

Sir George bowed a gracious assent to an amendment that was far from unpalatable to him, and when the numerous wants of the company, in the shape of spirit, lemons, and tobacco, had been supplied, Fothergill proceeded.

"I think, gentlemen, you all know why we are met here to-night; so I shall cut my remarks short. During the last year or two, Mr. Oliphant has been doing some very strange things, strange, offensive, and unjustifiable. Our village was a peaceable little place enough before he came to it; but for a long time he has considered it necessary to pry into everybody's concerns, manage people's business for them, and be the grand 'censor morum' of every household, finding out our faults or inventing faults for us, and then scolding or preaching, lecturing or hectoring us into amendment."

"Ay, he licks ye hollow at sarmonising, Mr. Truman, up hill or down," remarked Wideawake; "he hes twice as mich wind for t' job as iver ye hed, an' he niver breks t' trot, nauther."

"Order, Mr. Wideawake," said the chairman.

"Who is there that has not suffered from him?" continued Fothergill. "You, sir, and Mr. Wideawake here, have been brought before a court of law by him; Hawtrey and Mrs. Mansfield have been threatened and grossly insulted, Truman has been severely rated and 'cut;' all for paltry or imaginary offences. Down to the very boys, the villagers almost individually have sustained injury or insult from him—and then he must try forsooth to dragoon them into submission!—excuse me, Captain Highside, I mean no reflection on you; you only did your duty. To crown all, in the same domineering spirit he must turn his niece out of doors on one of the wildest nights ever known, without a moment's grace or preparation, and without even any reasonable cause. I shudder when I think of that terrible walk of hers through the snow."

"Yes, and Mrs. Oliphant—one of the most agreeable and ladylike women I ever met," said the baronet; "I consider his conduct in sending her off, without the slightest reason apparently, by far the worst thing he has done."

"Poor Kate!" sighed Harry. "What are we to do to him?"

"Have patience, Mr. Highside, for a minute," resumed Fothergill. "I know he would say, and very truly, that he did all this believing it to be right—I have observed that anything specially bad always is done in the name of justice : I know, too, that to a man of his wealth a certain influence is due ; but it must be freely given and not enforced."

" I really do not see why a man should have influence merely because he is rich, Fothergill," said the chairman ; " there are better men in this room than Jabez Oliphant. A man, who does not know his own grandfather, and whose father is only too well known, should not come back to his native village to give himself airs. He should go where he is not known."

" True, Sir George ; but with submission, and as a mere fact, large wealth always has a certain power. However, we are all tired of this domineering of his, and are agreed that he is not to be king over us any longer—not even to be old King Congo, Dick—if we can help it. And by leaguing against him, we can at least scotch the snake if we cannot kill it."

" Ay, he's a girt boa-constrictor 'at 'ud swallow us up, banes an' aw, if his mouth wor nobbut big enough ; an' aw acos he likes us sa weel !"

" Well, Mr. Fothergill," said Hawtrey, " we are thus far agreed ; we have to stop the nuisance. But let us have some practical suggestion as to the means."

" I had rather have left that to yourselves, gentlemen," replied William. " However, suppose we first try to get him struck off the commission. The loss of his office would be a great blow both to his pride and influence."

" True," cried every one ; " it would be capital : but how is it to be done ?"

" I think it might be done by a petition

influentially signed. The way he acted
when the public meeting was held about
him, must be our sheet anchor,—his ordering out the yeomanry and making them
charge. We must set forth how unneces-
sary any interference was, and how dreadful
the consequences might have been if—if
the yeomanry—what shall I say, Harry?"
he added, turning towards Highside with
a slyness which made all the company
laugh.

" Why, if Mr. Highside hedn't liked a
noggin o' brandy here at t' Red Lion better
than a brokken head on t' Green," said
Dick ; " an' nane sich a bad choice, nauther,
Mr. Highside.   Ye've cut yer wisdom teeth,
I can see."

" Come now, Fothergill, what could I
do ?" said Harry.   " You know I had only
two fellows with me, and as for that O'Cal-
laghan—"

"Oh, don't apologise for not having cut our throats, Harry," interrupted William; "one easily forgives a failure of that sort. The truth is it was a very foolish business, and we must make it out in our petition to be as foolish as we possibly can, throwing all the blame, of course, on Mr. Oliphant, and expressing very strongly our opinion that he is in consequence utterly unfit to have a seat on the bench. I'll word the thing if you like, and here are three magistrates who will sign it at once, I suppose—you, Sir George, Mr. Carlton, and myself. We can get almost all the justices who attend Stainton sessions to foot it; and if all persons present will do the same, and Dick here will undertake afterwards to go round with it in the village, why, I think we shall make out a pretty strong case for the interference of her Majesty's Secretary of State."

"I'll tak it round wi' pleasure," said Wideawake, "an' begow I willn't leave man, woman or child till I've gitten 'em to put their names tull it. Ye sall see now what I can do wi' 'em, though I'se nobbut a plain farmer."

"Yes, a horse-jobber, too, and a confoundedly sharp file at it!" said Fothergill; "you're forgetting that brown mare again. The horse-jobbing does more for you, Dick, than ever your farm did."

"Whya, whya, happen it does an' happen it doesn't. Yan cannot bear to see an honest penny ligging i' t' road, ye knaw, wi'out stooping to pick it up; yan 'ud be a born fool if yan could: for efter aw, brass is brass, as ye said yersel.—Mrs. Grandilugs, let's hev another noggin—an' try to put some gin in it this time, d'ye hear!— There's as mich distance atween t' drops o' spirit i' what they caw gin an' watter here,

as there is atween trouts i' a beck, Mr.
Truman. Efter ye've swallowed t' first
drop i' a mouthful o' watter, ye've to wait
hauf an hour afore ye come to t' next."

" I don't think, Fothergill," said Truman,
" that I can sign this petition myself. It
would be an act of revenge."

" But surely you do not think he was
right in the steps he took about the public
meeting ?"

" No, I think he acted very injudiciously,
as he has often done. But through all his
crotchets, he has intended to be both just
and generous ; only he is too dictatorial."

" And that's just what no gentleman can
stand, you know," said Harry. " If you've
a thoroughbred you must coax her, mustn't
you, Dick ? Fancy Jabez Oliphant trying
to dictate to my father there !"

" But he could not, Harry ; he could
not," said the baronet. " I despise him ;

and all he can do is not worth a moment's notice. But I don't understand what the parson there is thinking about : you surely will not desert us at a pinch, Truman,— refuse to sign, eh ?"

"I think Mr. Truman is right," said John Hawtrey. " As the clergyman of the place, he ought to live in peace with all men ; as indeed he does, bearing enmity to no living thing I could ever hear of, but the fish and the caterpillars in his garden, and I have no doubt he has long since found out the easiest means of killing these. However, I shall be glad to sign and give you a specimen of the church militant."

Truman was the only person present who declined to back the petition, and the latter having been decided on, he said rather doubtfully, "There is perhaps one thing which I could have approved."

"What is that? Let us have the clerical mite by all means," said Fothergill. "A hulking six-foot fellow like you, Truman, has no right to keep such a tender conscience. You should give it to some sickly girl, and get another."

"Girl, or conscience?" asked Harry. "Now, don't you know he is booked for Miss Norber, Fothergill, and she's no chicken? Wouldn't her nose grow sharper still if she thought old Truman was after anybody else!"

"Now, Harry," said the incumbent, making his stereotyped reply to badinage of this kind, "how absurd you are! Why, how can I marry on an income of seventy-two pounds four shillings and twopence? And then you know I'm too old by ten years."

"Not a bit too owd, Mr. Truman," remarked Dick; "don't ye knaw 'at women all'ays like chaps 'at hev hed a bit of experience? As to yer incomings, they aren't mich to be sure; twa three bits o' dealing i' horseflesh 'ud be worth mair nor aw t' boiling—that is," he added, hastily, "if they were varra lucky uns—I don't say all'ays, ye know. But I'll tell ye what, Mr. Truman; as ye hevn't mich yersel, ye owt to marry a lady wi' a fortun'; she's na business wi' sa mich brass, hes ony single lady, say I—she owt to share it wi' some fellow 'at can spend it for her like a gentleman. Dung isn't worth ought till it's spread, ye knaw, an' what's t' good o' letting it lig o' heaps?"

"Very good advice, Dick," said Hawtrey. "But what is your plan, Truman?"

"Well, could we dissolve this absurd society of Mr. Oliphant's for the Propagation of Virtue? It does a great deal of harm in the parish, I fear,—gives him an opportunity of interfering every-where."

"Hurrah, yes; that'll be another rap for him," shouted Harry, "and, by Jove, I'm ashamed of seeing my name on that prospectus. Aren't you, father? You're down too, you know."

"No, Harry," said the baronet, "I am not ashamed of anything I ever did—have no reason, sir: who is there that I need be afraid of? But as Mr. Truman thinks this society a failure, I shall be happy to take your votes about dissolving it."

"But can we dissolve it without summoning a formal meeting of the committee and Mr. Oliphant?" asked Fothergill.

"Why, sir, almost all the committee are present," said the chairman testily; "and we know, almost as well as if he were here, what that fellow Oliphant would say. We must count him as one vote against the proposition—that's all. I rule, sir, that we are perfectly competent to settle the question."

" And I propose, then, that this—this Virtue, or what you call it, be done away with," exclaimed Harry.

" This Society for the Propagation of Virtue, you mean, Harry, I suppose," said the chairman. " Very well ; is there any opposition to the motion ? Carried then without dissentients, and I declare the said society dissolved. What is the next proposition ?"

" Can you suggest anything yourself ?" inquired Fothergill, knowing the deference which the old baronet always expected.

" Why, no ; unless all here were to agree to take no further notice of him. Of course, I shall take none ; but it is for the rest of you to consider whether what this low fellow has done in the neighbourhood does not en-title him to be sent to Coventry by every one."

"A very good notion, Sir George," said Fothergill; "and besides cutting him, to make him ashamed of himself if we can, we ought to agree together, all who are here, to unite in opposing him if he attempts any further onslaught on any one in the district, whether rich or poor; and in that case, we ought to see if we cannot find some charge against himself and bring him before the magistrates; for that would be a harder blow to him than anything."

"In fact, we are to form ourselves into an Anti-Oliphant and Mutual Protection Society in place of the one we have just broken up? Well, I'll make one," said Hawtrey.

"Yes, and we are not to visit him."

"But if he wants a cart-horse or ought o' that sort," inquired the farmer, "I isn't to be shut off frae sarving him, if we can trade?   I might just as weel hev ony profit there's to be gitten out of him, as Isaiah Ducksberry, ivery bit."

" Yes, Dick ; and the more you can bite him, the better the present company will be pleased," replied Fothergill.

All except Truman having agreed on this point also, " Well, I propose," cried Harry, starting up, " that we appoint somebody to give him a taste of a stick, just as a finishing touch to all the rest.   Nobody can say he doesn't richly deserve it, after what he has done about his niece and Mrs. Mansfield."

" I'll be hanged if that isn't t' maist sensible proposition I've heard to-neght : wha wad ha thowt it o' *ye*, Maister Highside?" said Dick enthusiastically.   " Ye'll come out a topper for sense yet, ye'll see.   Let's give him a bit o' club-law an' hev done wi' it; I reckon nought o' bearing malice for a lang time. I wadn't harm him mich, ye knaw, acos he's an owd man—but a few blue wheals across t' back frae a good esh stick, or a couple o' black eyes wadn't hurt him, an' it 'ud tak t' nonsense out of him better nor ought."

"And I'll be the man to do it, if you like. Hurrah!" cried Harry.

"Nay, ye'd be too savage, Maister Highside," answered Wideawake. "It wad hev to be done varra deftly an' judgmatically, an' by somebody who's hed a gay bit of experience i' that way. Now, there's mysel, if ye like: I've hed mony a feght up an' down an' I ken better nor maist folk how to lig on gently if I dunnot want to hurt a chap ower mich."

"No, it will not do, Harry," said Fothergill decisively. "It would be disgraceful to strike an old man."

"Very, very," echoed Hawtrey and Truman.

"I myself, as a person occupying a certain position in the county, cannot agree to this, gentlemen," said the chairman. "If anything of the kind happens, you must take the entire responsibility on yourselves."

As all were against Harry's proposal therefore, except Dick, it was rejected ignominiously.

"Well, it caps me," grumbled Dick, "'at ye can't see 'at a lile bit o' stick at yance is baith easier an' mair straightforrard like, than sa mich doubling about him an' sulking ower him. He'd like it better hissel, I'se sure he wad. Howiver, as ye're aw again' us, hev ye ought sensible to propose insteead, Mr. Hawtrey? Ye're a gerund-grinder, an' owt to know some'at about naughty childer, an' how to tak their wickedness out of 'em."

"I certainly should like to propose one thing in addition," said the schoolmaster, " by which I think we should revenge ourselves on Mr. Oliphant in the noblest way possible, and which would at the same time supply a want that has long been discreditable to ourselves. Mr. Oliphant has hitherto very generously increased Mr. Truman's miserable stipend to one hundred and fifty pounds a year, but now, out of pique at his conduct, sends him back to his old allowance, thinking no doubt he can either keep him poor or make him rich at his pleasure. Now let us show him that he is mistaken in this notion ; let us raise a handsome subscription to increase the endowment of the living and give the incumbent a chance of existing independent of every one. What do you say ?"

"I say that it is an excellent and a very generous revenge," said Fothergill, "and if

Sir George will head the subscription list, I will follow him, though I am not a rich man, with a hundred guineas."

The baronet, who was rather stingy, had been changing colour a good deal during Hawtrey's remarks, and was fumbling nervously about his pockets, as if he were trying to button them up from all possible chance of assault : but he was fairly caught in a trap by Fothergill, and felt that he could not demur without lowering the family dignity, which he valued even more than his money.

" Well, really, Mr. Fothergill—if the proposition is quite agreeable to the company ; it is quite a surprise to us, and—and naturally some one in the room may object," he said, with no very good grace.

But Fothergill swept the baronet's feeble hope away by asking the company at once if there was any opposition. Then he turned to him with a look of cynical pleasure and remarked that all seemed in favour of the motion.

"Yes—yes," said Sir George; "then I will give—that is, I have much pleasure in giving the same amount as yourself, Mr. Fothergill." He knew that this was the least which would be expected from him, for he was a far richer man than William.

Carlton too promised a hundred pounds, Hawtrey fifty, Harry (who was more generous than his father) twenty, and Dick five; the latter accompanying his subscription with some advice to Truman about his ministrations.

Before the meeting separated, the amount promised reached four hundred and fifty pounds; and, as Fothergill walked home with the schoolmaster, he could not forbear a sarcastic laugh.

"That was a happy stroke of yours,

Hawtrey, about the endowment. Is it not amusing that what justice and generosity might have begged for years without effect, a little pique has accomplished at once? Yet these men will go home and think they have a right to sounder sleep for having performed a munificent action. I know I think so of myself."

"It was certainly amusing to see Sir George's face after you had fairly caught him," said Hawtrey. "In spite of his wrath at Mr. Oliphant, he would gladly have compounded with you to let him slip out of the room."

"Well, let us be thankful that we have done a good work, no matter what the motives were. We shall easily raise the subscriptions to seven or eight hundred pounds, you will see. But it would be a curious question to inquire how many will give from seeing the baronet's name at the head of the list, or from hatred of Mr. Oliphant, and how few from a love of Mother Church or Father Truman."

And Fothergill was right, for the subscription ran up soon to more than the amount he talked of: and this, safely invested at five per cent., made Truman as happy as it made Mr. Oliphant indignant; for the latter very justly considered the matter only as a kind of revenge which the Reinsber carles were taking on himself.

Nor was his anger lessened on his being curtly informed in a note from Fothergill, beginning 'Sir' and ending 'Your obedient servant,' that his pet society was maliciously blown to atoms without his having even been told it was in danger. The same note briefly stated that most of the gentlemen about, including the writer, disagreed so entirely with Mr. Oliphant in much he had done, that they had determined to hold no further intercourse with him. But his wrath reached its climax as he read on and found they intended to strike him off the commission, for Fothergill thought it only fair to tell him their purpose. And this was the village for which he had done so much!

The whole thing came on him like a thunderbolt; for, wrapped up in his great projects, he scarcely knew that he had excited any deep or permanent ill-will in the neighbourhood. Yet there it was, in black and white, this signal piece of ingratitude. He was not so crushed, however, as not to make a hard fight about the petition; but it was signed by almost every one, and was so well backed up by arguments that within a fortnight he had ceased to be a magistrate.

Then he sulked in his tent, like Achilles, with unbroken pride and dauntless fortitude, only that he could see no way either of showing his resentment or of prosecuting his philanthropic schemes ; for all the village seemed set against him, and even the poor people to whom he gave his six-pences were scarcely civil. He felt supreme contempt indeed for the coalition which had cut the ground from under him so suddenly, and he kept himself sternly apart, brooding over his wrongs. But contempt breaks no bones, and the conspirators only laughed at the airs of their dethroned monarch.

CHAPTER XII.

A CHARACTER—AFTER MACHIAVELLI AND THE HISTORIANS.

THUS fell Jabez Oliphant in the third year of his reign. In examining his conduct we shall find scarcely anything that can be ascribed to good fortune. It was not by chance or any accident of birth, but by his own genius, that he attained the sovereignty of Reinsber, amid all the intrigues of the Saints, and to the surprise of its inhabitants ; and it was only by the greatest coolness and heroic resolution that he maintained so long what he had thus acquired. His administration was a splendid one. Great works were undertaken, nuisances suppressed, the arts encouraged, morality and the laws enforced. Nor was he content, like many princes, with prescribing their duty to his subjects; but he was himself in humility, courteousness, and sobriety, their chief exemplar. In business matters he was exact, in donatives munificent. It has been said that the perfect prince should combine the qualities of the fox and the lion, and we see the remark exemplified in Mr. Oliphant; for in the first part of his reign he depended for success on shrewdness of argument and sagacious reasoning, while later, when he felt his power established, he acted the lion's part, not caring to disguise his strength but employing it to strike terror into any malignant individuals that opposed him.

His deposition affords a melancholy instance of the frailty of all human grandeur and the instability of fortune. He fell partly by a sudden coalition of men whom he had vanquished singly ; but more from the intractable nature of his subjects and their lamentable incapacity for appreciating undiluted virtue. His danger from the latter defect he had foreseen, and against it had intended to make four different provisions : viz., in the first place, by showing his people, through example and education, how glorious and beautiful such virtue is ; secondly, by attaching to her interests every person of any influence in his dominions ; thirdly, by acquiring so much power as to make it impossible for any one to resist her voice through him ; and, lastly, by publishing in a collected form, and with numerous additions, the arguments which he had employed at various times in favour of morality or against vice.

Two of these precautionary measures

he had already carried out fully, and the third in part: for he had himself set the example, and had called a hundred refining and ennobling agencies into being in the village; while he had either allured all the neighbouring gentry to the side of virtue by placing their names on the committee of his great society, or had shown them that they could not transgress her dictates with impunity. He had also acquired much power already and was rapidly gaining more, as was shown by the fears of the conspirators and the sudden measures they thought it necessary to adopt against him. The only precaution he had not yet found time for (and this was a circumstance he regretted' more than anything) was the publication above mentioned; nor after his downfall did he ever care to go on with this great work.

As to the conspiracy, he told me himself

that he always considered it a mere accident which no sagacity could have foreseen ; it was like the premature fall of
snow, thirty days before the usual time,
which led to the ruin of Napoleon in his
Russian campaign.   But Mr. Oliphant
assured me that if this coalition had not
happened exactly at the time it did, or had
not been so sudden and totally unexpected,
he would have been able effectually to
crush it.

Upon a thorough review, therefore, of his
conduct and actions, I cannot reproach him
with having omitted any precautions ; and I
feel that he merits being proposed as a model
to all who, in modern times, are ambitious of
ruling such a principality as that of Reinsber.

It is in himself and his own courage alone
that a prince should seek refuge in misfortune ; and it only remains to depict the
career of Mr. Oliphant in his retirement.

BOOK THE LAST.

THE PRINCE IN RETIREMENT.

CHAPTER I.

MR. OLIPHANT IN PRIVATE LIFE.

THE little village of Reinsber had resumed its peace of mind, and everything there went on just as if the great
Jabez Oliphant had never existed or existed
no longer. The heavy-headed carles had
begun to forget his splendid despotism and
his desperate efforts at philanthropy, and
were relapsing fast, with natural gravitation,
into the habits and vices of their forefathers.
His lessons in civilisation were gone like a

dream, and the drains were beginning to be odorous once more, and the middens to extend themselves pleasantly over the footpaths. The stream carolled merrily through the village, as of yore, and the gobbling old turkey-cock—without a competitor in his glories now—paraded the quiet streets in a morning still. Only, on the very rare occasions when their deposed monarch passed them with his dignified step, the groups of rustics would suspend their chatter till he was gone, or give a sly laugh under their breath as he disappeared.

The carriage-drive to the Hall had grown very green, and the hinges of the gates required oiling frequently; for none of the neighbouring gentry ever went near the house now, except a few from some distance who had not joined the coalition : and even these only paid occasional state-calls which were very formidable things ; for Mr. Oliphant, though extremely courteous, stood on his dignity more than ever, and pertinaciously confined the conversation to the state of the weather and the crops, or the health of the other's family. It was a relief to both sides when the decorous quarter of an hour was over.

An occasional visit of a day or two from Lord Stainmore alone broke the monotony of Mr. Oliphant's life at this period; and so well did the able viscount lament the other's misfortunes, so cunningly did he hint at the way in which he should model his own administration of the family estates, when he came to them, on that of Jabez, that he charmed the latter into making a new will in his favour. No doubt this was partly owing to the fact that Mr. Oliphant conceived that a member of his family had done his lordship a grievous injury, and partly because, in spite of several attempts after Kate's departure, he found that none of his other relatives came up to the high standard of excellence he required. But he also said that, in his opinion, the friend of your choice had a stronger claim on you than those whom mere accident had made your relatives; and that a man of large fortune was bound to leave it to those who would do most good with it.

Accordingly he bequeathed only a few legacies to his relations, and all the rest of his money, with the exception of large donations to various charitable institutions, to Lord Stainmore. Kate's name was never even mentioned in the document: to her uncle she had ceased to exist.

To do Stainmore justice, he had nothing to do with suggesting such a will, and never even knew of its existence, though, being always embarrassed and in advance of his income, he would probably have been delighted enough to hear that such a golden windfall was destined for him.

During the long years of almost unbroken solitude that followed his retirement from public life, Mr. Oliphant supported his reverses with staid and melancholy dignity. His habits were very regular and methodical. He rose, ate, worked, slept and took exercise by the clock. Like Diocletian and other great men under similar circumstances, he spent his time mainly in gardening, an occupation congenial to active minds that have had much to do with important affairs and the management of men. He averred that the garden is an empire in miniature, only pleasanter than other empires because you may train, lop and transplant your subjects as you please or think best for their good, without either fearing insurrection or being thwarted by opposition. In fact, according to the popular accounts, Jabez often went so far, when alone, as to address long and eloquent speeches to his assembled cauliflowers, or ask his tulips to dinner and—receiving them with winning bows, smiles, and all the royal courtesy for which he was so distinguished, and which was all the more necessary in the case of guests that had so little to say for themselves—explain his policy to them at length and aloud. The eaves-droppers of the village said they had heard him holding dialogue by the hour together with his rose-trees ; remonstrating with them in touching terms on the gross im-propriety of their conduct ; raising and answering a hundred objections for them ; threatening them with summary execution, either by taking up or turning out, if they did not improve ; and finally, when they still remained obstinate and his anger could no longer be restrained, ordering in firm tones the neighbouring gooseberry bushes to charge and quell this atrocious insurrection.

Sometimes, generally going and returning the same way, he drove out in solitary state ; his large open carriage with the pair of splendid bays, their silver harness and accompaniments of blue coachman in front and two blue footmen behind, being the admiration of the few rustics who happened to be wandering about the quiet lanes. On these occasions he might usually be seen leaning back in his seat with folded arms, and sad, abstracted look—a grand proud old man, whom misfortune might break but could not bend. But whatever thoughts occupied him, he never omitted to lift his hat with magnificent courtesy to the meanest beggar who saluted the grandeur of his equipage. More rarely he walked a mile or two beyond the limits of his own grounds, and then he showed the generosity still existing in him by rewarding with sixpence, as "a good boy," any youngster who touched his cap to him : indeed it became the fashion among the sharp Reinsber boys, when supplies of pocket-money fell short, to go and look for Old King Congo, as they still irreverently styled him.

At six to a minute he dined,—always alone ; though, either in faint remembrance of former times or in anticipation of guests that never came, covers were invariably laid for three. He always made his appearance at table in full dress, and was as exact in the matter as if he had been expecting a roomful of ladies ; for he used to say with a smile that he had never in his life met any better company than himself, so why should he omit this mark of respect even when he was alone ? From the same feeling I suppose, he was almost punctilious about the etiquette and ceremonies to be observed towards him by the servants, and was very angry at any breach of such propriety.

After dinner he read, or busied himself for hours in ticketing, arranging and retouching his voluminous state-papers and correspondence, of all which he had kept beautifully written copies—the sole remains, alas! of his labours for the public weal at Reinsber. His favourite literature, after the Prince, seems to have been history, political economy, and the Orations of Demosthenes, to whom he confessed himself indebted for all that was great in his own speeches. Romance he abhorred, for he said that, even in his own experience, he had known facts far stranger than any fiction; and what was the use of creating fanciful sorrows when there were only too many real ones in the world already?

Mr. Oliphant's sole retainer and confidant—

Faithful found
Among the faithless, faithful only he—

was Tommy Doolittle, to whom he frequently enlarged on various points of state-craft and philosophy ; putting the matter in the form of axiom or instance, as he thought would best suit his hearer's capacity at the moment.   These interviews generally took place either in the grocer's shop or the Hall garden, where Tommy, on one errand or another, became a frequent visitor, watching Mr. Oliphant as he plied his spade or pruning-knife, and sometimes lending a little assistance.

Then Jabez talked copiously, and Tommy listened ; in fact, for all purposes of reply, Mr. Oliphant might almost as well have had Hercules from the Green to talk to as Tommy. But, if the latter's part in the play was small, it must be owned he did that part re-markably well.   He would stand by for half a day, drinking in the flowing words, and, lest he should miss any of them, keeping his eye absolutely nailed on the oracular fountain from which they streamed, never tired or restless, with such delighted deference all the time—so quiet, yet so intelligent and attentive with a 'yes' or 'no' or respectful admiration at the proper place, that any mortal man whatever with a heart (let alone a lover of his species like Mr. Oliphant) would have thought it a sin and a shame to stint Tommy in his morning draught of wisdom. He was no toady either; he asked no favours, and wanted none. It was an honest admiration, in which he had long since completely lost himself, of Mr. Oliphant's wonderful superiority to all the world in wealth, virtues, capacity, and condescension. To Tommy Jabez was a new and rich El Dorado, to which he himself (happy little grocer) had the only key, and in which he could revel alone. With his friends in the village, or with strangers, it was charming to hear

Tommy's mysterious references to what "a certain friend of his" had said, or "a very rich man he knew," or "a most influential personage with whom he talked occasionally." In a word, Jabez was Tommy's Imperial Guard, on which he could always depend for winning the battle when he pleased.

Only a few fragments of Mr. Oliphant's discourses with Tommy have survived ; and these were preserved simply through Doolittle's having been so much struck with them that he committed them to writing soon after they were delivered. The majority were mere scraps, scarcely worth transcribing, such as the following :

"A star with us is a sun elsewhere. I have known persons, who were thought very little of in the country, be considered magnates of the very first order in London.

"I did not take up oratory till I was

advanced in life; but I soon found out that the secret of all public speaking is to have something to say, to remember what it is, and to say it briefly."

Occasionally, however, these oracular utterances assumed larger dimensions :

" Hark how yon blackbird sings, Doolittle !" was his remark one day : " I'll be bound he is the happiest of the three, yet he has not a rag to his back, and he has a larger family to keep than you. You do not sing like that, to cheer Mrs. Doolittle's heart when you are weighing sugar, eh ?"

" I never think of it, somehow, sir ; but I do sometimes join in a temperance melody," answered the smirking little man.

" Well, all Mr. Blackbird's songs are temperance melodies, but they are as lively as the best bacchanalian chants. I am quite of his opinion, Mr. Doolittle ; I think poor men should be happier than the rich."

"His opinion, sir! But is that his opinion?"

"Certainly, or he would not be so cheerful when he has nothing."

"But is he not mistaken, sir, if he thinks so?"

"Not a bit," replied Jabez, impressively. "Gold is the heaviest of metals, and grows a burden at last. Then, the rich are only the poor man's stewards : they provide him with bread, with roads, ships and railways to travel by, parks and palaces to visit. He has physicians at their cost when he is sick, and a good house when he is old. He does not know the tax-gatherer's face, or the flatterer, for 'why should the poor be flattered ?' His friends are true friends, and it is worth no one's while to wrong him. Believe me, he has many advantages."

Once only did Mr. Oliphant's pride break down so far as to make any direct reference to himself. It was one summer afternoon when Tommy went to see him in the garden. After some conversation, Jabez said in a rather husky voice : "I have been this morning by the river and on the scars, Mr. Doolittle, visiting all the favourite haunts of my school-days. I had not been to look at them since Kate—well, since there was the break-up at the Hall."

"It must have been very pleasant," suggested Tommy.

"Pleasant! no, sir," replied Jabez with a sharp voice and a keen look at the little man ; "it was very painful ; I have scarcely got over it yet."

"I should have thought, sir, the difference between now and the time when you were a boy——"

"Yes, yes," interrupted Mr. Oliphant ;

" all this was pleasant enough at first when I came back to Reinsber. I visited these places very often till a year or two ago—with a companion—a sympathetic companion—and the smell of the hawthorn and the sight of the old caves and pools always made a child of me again with delight,—in fact, they made children of both of us. This time, somehow the things failed utterly—like a drug that you take too often, I suppose. I was a fool for going, and came back very sad. One grows older, Doolittle ; and one's money scarcely does one as much good as you would think."

" Oh, sir !" remonstrated the grocer, with a timid, admiring glance round him.

" Well, yes ; it is all mine," said Jabez, speaking in reply to the look, and resting one foot on the spade as he looked round, himself. Then he went on slowly and musingly, more to himself than his audience : "But it is all very little, as I was thinking to-day, and have often thought before, if it does not make one happy. I do not know what I may appear to others, but to myself I seem to have spent the labour of a lifetime utterly in vain. For five-and-forty years my life might be summed up in one word—toil, toil with an object. For that object I worked in the dingy counting-house like a slave, early and late, summer and winter : to that I sacrificed my youth and my manhood : for that I neglected my acquaintance, gave up my holidays, postponed my pleasures till I could take my fill of them—now. It seems centuries to look back upon, that time of figures, and work, and money-getting, and I should never have got through it but for the memories of sweet Reinsber primrose banks that haunted me through it all, and spurred me on with hopes of happiness at the end.   Well, it was over at last.   I had got my golden apples, and lo ! I find them ashes.   I thought of making all these stupid people happy, and of being happy myself in doing it, and they will not let me.—It is rather hard to fail when one has reached the topmost step of the ladder, is it not ?   However, so it is with me.   My dreams are gone, and my friends—such as I ever had—nay, my very relatives ; and at seventy I sit alone among the ruins of my wasted life, a poor, miserable old man, with regrets for the past and despair of the future as my sole companions."

Not a few tears had fallen from the old man's eyes as he mused on in this way, but he had turned his face from Doolittle. The latter was much affected, but did not know what to say to comfort him.   After a silence of a few minutes, he asked :

“ But could you not try some other amusement or something new, sir ?”

“ I am too old to take up other pursuits now, or to make new friends : and I find I have put off my amusements till I have lost all capacity for them, Mr. Doolittle. No, the tree must stand as it is bent. There is nothing left but to die hard, as they will not let me be soft and kind to them ; and I shall die hard enough, with hired hands to nurse me, and no friend to close my eyes—nothing but greedy expectant relatives, waiting like crows till the breath is out of my body to pounce on my leavings. But they’ll be disappointed—they shall be disappointed.”

“ O sir, but couldn’t you be reconciled to Mrs. Holden ? She was kind to you and everybody,” said the honest little grocer, all in a flurry of haste and trepidation ; for he knew he was venturing on dangerous ground, and yet was most anxious to remedy the unhappiness of his friend if possible.

Mr. Oliphant had never been angry with Tommy before; but now he absolutely flamed indignation, and his wrath recalled him to his harder self.

"Mr. Doolittle," he exclaimed, "if I sometimes allow you to talk freely with me" (this was rather hard, by the way, on the little man whom Mr. Oliphant's volubility condemned to almost perpetual silence), "that is no reason why you should become impertinent. I will not have my niece back, and that is enough. She has paid you to speak for her, I suppose," he added, contemptuously. Then he went on in a careless tone: "One's griefs cannot be very great, after all, when one can talk of them so much, and I suppose all men have some annoyance or other. But

I am rather tired, and shall go in. Good afternoon."

And for some weeks Jabez was more distant than usual with Tommy, and never at any time referred again to his sorrows. But he brooded on them proudly and secretly all the same, and, in spite of his wealth, I imagine there were few men in England more resolutely miserable than Jabez Oliphant.

CHAPTER II.

MR. OLIPHANT'S LAST STRUGGLE FOR POWER.

ONLY once did Mr. Oliphant make an effort to recover his former influence at Reinsber.   This was when a gentleman named Elton bought a large estate in the neighbourhood, and came to reside there permanently.   He was a cotton manufacturer from Lancashire, and, like Mr. Oliphant, ' a self-made man,' who had amassed a fortune, which he wished to enjoy in his old age.   Now it struck Jabez, who had by no means grown contented with his forced solitude and inactivity, that he might possibly be able to secure the friendship of a new-comer whose antecedents were so similar to his own, and whose influence, if judiciously employed, might perhaps almost replace Mr. Oliphant in the authoritative position he once occupied. A throne is worth recovering, even if it can only be regained by the forces of a neighbouring potentate.

Accordingly, one day in April, Mr. Oliphant dressed himself with great care, and drove to the Grange, to make his call on Mr. Elton. The latter was a short, rather stout man, with a mass of curly grey hair, a round face, and a good-humoured twinkle in his eye. He was a true ' Lancashire lad ' still, and straightforward, almost to roughness, in his manners. His wife, a barber's daughter (for John Elton had married long before he was even a foreman at the mills he afterwards owned), was plump, rosy, and good-natured, with a showy dress and a profusion of jewelry; but the discreet silence she maintained was perhaps the best jewel about her.

"I say, Mr. Oliphant," said Elton, when they had conversed on ordinary topics for some time, "can you tell me how country gentlemen do manage to pass their time? I've made lots of money by cotton, you know, just as you have done by tea, and so Betsy here would have us to turn into fashionable folk, and me to be a country squire; so, as I always give in to her, here I've been these six weeks; but it passes me how they get through the day."

"Why, do you find some difficulty yourself?"

"Difficulty! I should think so. No business, for I've given that up to my son, and don't intend to make any more money

—no telegraph—no penny papers—no clerks rushing in! I get on pretty well at night, for my wife and I play double dummy till nine; or if she can't play, I take the three dummies myself, right hand against left, and sometimes for variety left against right, you know; and then at nine there's the *Times*. But the day-time is the deuce. By sitting up very late over my paper, I manage to snooze away the greater part of the morning; but still there's always six mortal hours to be got through before tea-time. It is my opinion, sir, that a country life is all humbug."

"Could you not spend some of your time in gardening, as I do, or altering your house or grounds?"

"What's the good of altering when they're both as neat as they can be? *We* never lived in as grand a house before, did we, Betsy? And then, as to gardening, why, I've an old Scotchman who does it all for a hundred a year, a deal better than I could do it."

"Are you fond of riding or walking, then ?"

"Never learned to ride in my life, and a fall with my weight would be no joke, Mr. Oliphant.   But I'm fond enough of strolling out for a mile or so, if there's anything to see ; only that's just it; there is nothing to see here except rocks, and rivers, and trees, which may do very well for verse-writers to cackle over, but don't give plain folk much to think about.   I'd rather see a new cotton mill, or a fly-wheel, myself. There's brain and power in that."

"You must shoot, Mr. Elton."

"Nay, that's greater humbug than ever. Imagine a man of seventeen stone trotting for a day together over the roughest land in the country, and all to bag three or four poor birds, that one might buy without the trouble for half the money they cost in preserving, to say nothing of one's day's wages. Of course I've taken a moor, like other fools that want to be fashionable, but every grouse of my own costs me half a guinea ; and I can buy them in Manchester market for six shillings a brace ! Hares and rabbits the same."

" Could you not improve your land ?"

" And lose money by it, as not understanding it, eh ?" said the Lancashire lad with a shrewd wink at Mr. Oliphant. "Thank you, if I've given up money-making, I don't want to lose it. But now, talking of that, it strikes me, sir, there are mines on mines of gold lying in these hills here, in the limestone, and lead, and slate that nobody seems to have thought of working. Don't you think it would be a capital 'spec' to open some of them out—

just for amusement, you know ?   What do you think of the thing as a practical man, Mr. Oliphant ?   I should say it would pay well."

"I dare say it might; but I confess I should be sorry to see our beautiful valley broken up by such things."

"Ah, I'm not sentimental, as I think I said.   And one must have something to do. I should like to try it; but the cost of coal would be a heavy item."

"There is one thing to be said in favour of your scheme, that you would at all events be giving employment to many poor people, which no doubt would be very gratifying to you, Mr. Elton," replied Jabez, paving the way for the introduction of his own grievances.

"Oh, of course," answered Elton carelessly, "employing them would save one something in rates, as you say; but it couldn't be much. Poor-rates heavy here, I suppose?"

"Rather heavy—I have no doubt, Mr. Elton," said Jabez, plunging into his subject, "that, as a large employer of labour, you are much interested in the welfare and improvement of the working classes?"

"Well, I don't know, I'm sure: my idea is, that if a fellow can't help himself, he is not worth helping; so that I think the best thing one can do for the working classes is just to leave 'em alone."

"But still I have little doubt your kind actions would belie your words." Then Mr. Oliphant hurried on, without waiting for an answer: "Now, I have tried my best to do what good I could in Reinsber, but you would be astonished to hear how all my efforts have been opposed and thwarted."

"Don't go on with them, then, that's all,

Mr. Oliphant.   Leave the beggars to their fate, and smoke your pipe in peace."

"I should have been truly glad to live at peace with every one; but the ignorance, the crotchetiness, the obstinacy of all, both rich and poor, in this place, are amazing, sir. You are a stranger and unprejudiced; and I should very much like your opinion on these transactions; for, if I am not greatly mistaken, you will see that I have been right in every single particular, and have been most unjustly treated.   I have a sort of short summary of these affairs here; and as there is the documentary evidence on both sides, you will be able, if I were to read it to you, to form a fair judgment on the matter."

Mr. Oliphant pulled with great difficulty out of the pockets of his surtout two long and thick bundles of papers, and laid them on the table.   John Elton gave a rude whistle of dismay at the sight, and ex-claimed, with a humorous twinkle in his eyes : " Good gracious, Mr. Oliphant ! why, they are either of them bigger than my big ledger."

" One can scarcely hope to get at truth easily in this world," replied Jabez with a sigh ; " there is usually a shell about it that is very hard to crack."

" And the kernel is often so small when you get at it, that it's not worth your trouble or the risk of breaking your teeth."

" I trust you will allow me to read a part of them," said Mr. Oliphant, almost humbly.

" Then you must come to dinner every day for a month, and we'll take them by bits in the afternoons. It will pass on the day till double-dummy time, won't it, Betsy ?"

Mr. Oliphant did not know whether to

take the proposal seriously or not "I
should be very glad if I could amuse you
during the time you find hanging so heavily
on your hands. But by hearing them, you
will at all events know what treatment a
philanthropist may expect at Reinsber, and
will even, if I may form a judgment of your
character, be disposed to assist me."

"No, no, Mr. Oliphant," replied Elton,
seriously and kindly. "We shall be delighted to see you at the Grange whenever
you choose to come and dine with us ; but
as to entering into bygone quarrels, whether they are yours or any man's, you must
really excuse me. There's nothing to be
got out of them but botheration. Let
them rest, man, among other lumber, and
don't disturb them. I should do so with
my own, and I've had a few quarrels in my
time ; but the only thing I wish now is to
forget them. As to amusement," he con-

tinued, pulling a comical face, "do you know, I should prefer the mines and lime-kilns; and if you are inclined to join me in the venture, I shall be very glad. Or what do you say to getting the telegraph to Reinsber, to tell us every morning a little of what is going on in the world? Or a railway up the valley? For any of these things, I'm your man."

"I have really tried so hard to improve Reinsber, Mr. Elton, and have met with such bad success, that I have no heart to attempt anything else at present." And Mr. Oliphant rose to go, much disappointed that his scheme had come to nothing.

"Well, remember you've promised to come to dinner whenever you like. I never give invitations without meaning them. We feed at one, pat. I've bought some silver spoons for the first time in my life, but I won't be so fashionable as to dine late.   Plain leg of mutton, or round of beef—something of that sort.   Hope you'll come."

So Mr. Oliphant gathered up his papers and drove off, to brood once more over his Utopia of the past; while Elton, scarcely less visionary, amused himself with projects for turning Reinsber at a profit into a little Cottonopolis.

CHAPTER III.

NEARLY four years had gone by since Mr. Oliphant was driven from public life, when two ruffianly-looking fellows were sitting smoking at the mouth of a little cave which lay close to one of the lonely hill roads above Reinsber. Their faces were blackened, and they were armed with bludgeons, while one of them had the butt of a pistol peeping from his coat-pocket, and the other a knife. It was about seven o'clock in the evening, and bright moonlight; but the darkness of the cave-mouth effectually screened them

from the observation of any chance passers-
by, while they could command from their
position a view of the road for a considerable distance each way.   In the cave, which
was entered by a low narrow passage, there
was a smouldering fire of turf.

There could be little doubt that the
scoundrels were there on some errand of
blood.   Yet, how incongruous such a purpose seemed to the place and the time!
The long masses of the hills, huger and
more weird than in the daytime, loomed
up on this side and that in the moonlight,
and looked like a score of giants gone to
their rest and laid in state, each one by
himself; while in the fantastic play of
light and shadow on the grey cliffs that
flanked them, there were strange forms of
genii, or spirit mourners, in dumb attend-
ance on the mighty dead.   In the valley
below, as far as the eye could reach, a bed

of mist lay like a sea, with here and there a detached hill piercing the white expanse, and presenting the appearance of a dark island or abutting promontory. There were few trees visible, but on them not a twig or a dead leaf moved. There was absolutely no wind and no sound, except the faint monotonous murmur of the rivulet in the low ground a mile or two away. A sort of holy calm seemed to have taken possession of all nature, and had banished for the time (one might have thought) both the tumult of the world and the evil passions of men.

"Rayther ower breght for our job, isn't it, Tom?" was the reflection of the shorter man of the two, as they conversed in a low voice.

"Now, thou isn't turning soft about it, Tony? That won't do wi' me," said the other, significantly touching the butt of his pistol; "besides, it's thy business, is this."

"Nay, I'se noan flaid, but I'se be glad when it's ower."

"Well, I willn't say but it's natteral, t' first time thou's hed ought to do wi' sich things. Tak a sup o' t' bottle to wakken thy pluck."

Tony complied, and then remarked: "Well, we'll sattle *him*, ony how." |

"Then it's decided 'at we finish him?"

"Begow, I'se finish him, I knaw, if I yance git at him—a cursed owd tyrant! Thou's turning soft now."

"Not I," said the taller man, with a scornful laugh; "dead men tell noa tales."

"He's a lang time coming."

"Thou doesn't think he could gang back ony other way, does ta? Thou sud knaw t' country."

"I knaw ivery yerd on't, an' I tell thee he'll come back this way."

"If he doesn't, I'se be mad."

"Whisht! Isn't yon somebody."

"Ay, it's him. Now let's gang an' meet him. Look slippy wi' thee."

"I think I wadn't use t' pistol, Tom; they'll hear it a mile to-neght, an' we'se be chased."

"Thee tell thy granny—and don't let thy hand shak sa mich."

Accordingly they sprang up, and advanced to meet the pedestrian who was approaching, and who was no other than Mr. Oliphant on his return from a long walk by himself. They came loungingly up, but the country was so quiet that he had no suspicion of their design till they were close to him and he saw their blackened faces.

"A fine neght, Mr. Oliphant," said the

fellow who was called Anthony, in a sneer-
ing tone; "ye're too grand a gentleman to
remember me, I've na doubt; but ye'll
knaw me better by and by."

"What do you mean, fellows?" said
Jabez, much alarmed, and raising his stick
to guard himself.

"We'll show ye that in a minute," said
the scoundrel, rushing on him with his
knife.

The brave old man, however, who knew
something of the art of self-defence, suc-
ceeded in warding off the blows of both
the men, and in fighting his way back to
the wall. Against this he planted himself,
shouting for assistance as hard as he could;
and he even found an opportunity to
exclaim: "What do you want, fellows? I
will give you all I have about me, if you'll
stand off."

"We want yer blood, ye owd divil, an'

we'll hev it," said the shorter ruffian, striking at him with the knife after each sentence. These blows, however, Mr. Oliphant also parried. But shortly afterwards, hearing a horse coming up at full
speed, the men rushed on him together,
and brought him to the ground by a blow
on the head. Then, while the fellow who
struck it set to work hastily rifling the old
man's pockets, the other, who was evidently
more intent on murder than plunder, gave
him a terrible thrust with his knife. The
near approach of the horseman, however,
obliged them the next moment to desist.

"It's only yan, Tony; we'll sattle him
too, if he doesn't gang quietly about his
business. Now stand firm," said the taller
scoundrel, drawing his pistol.

"Wha are *ye?* an' what are ye doing?"
said the horseman, riding right up to them,
and in stentorian tones, which poor Mr.

Oliphant, who was not quite insensible, recognised as Dick Wideawake's. Dick had been on one of his horse-jobbing expeditions, and this was his nearest road to Sandy Topping from Reinsber.

"What's that to thee?" said the man called Tom, cocking his pistol. "Mind yer ain business, ye big Yorkshire stirk, and gang on yer way quietly, or ye'll happen rue it."

The shade of the wall had hitherto prevented Dick from seeing the prostrate body of Mr. Oliphant, but now that gentleman, fearing the farmer might take advice which seemed remarkably prudent under the circumstances, gave a faint cry of "Help, help, Mr. Wideawake!"

"What, it's Mr. Oliphant, is it?" roared the farmer. "Ye murderin' divils!" And the gigantic dalesman, without a thought of the consequences to himself, spurred his horse on the fellow in a moment—his short thick hunting-whip uplifted in a ponderous hand that did not mean to strike twice. Dick owed his life, however, to his horse, which had more discretion than himself, and shied at the flash of the pistol; the ball, consequently, only carried away one of the farmer's luxuriant light curls, just above his ear. The next instant the whip handle came down on the ruffian's temple with a fury that broke the stock, and dropped the man to the ground like a stone.

"Now, then, for ye, ye scamp!" cried Dick, charging at the other fellow with a shout, which, like a wild Indian's war cry, both showed the farmer's thorough enjoyment of the skirmish, and called attention to valour that was too remarkable to pass unobserved. But the robber, though he had a knife, fled from the huge and furious

centaur, Dick charging after him and lash-
ing him on the head with the remains of
his whip.   So fast did the fellow run in his
fright, however, that Dick would have had
great difficulty in stopping him before he
sprang over the wall, which was very low
a few yards further on, if by a lucky
thought he had not twisted the long whip-
lash round the man's neck, and then pulled
it so tight as to stop and nearly strangle
him.   A single blow from the farmer's
mutton fist settled the rest of the business,
and Dick sprang off his horse by the man's
side, an easy victor.

"There!   Ye'll think twice, young man,
afore ye fight wi' Dick Wideawake again.
What, ye've a knife, hev ye, ye scamp?
Leave hod, or I'll mash yer head in wi'
yan blow;" and the farmer without more
ado shook the knife out of the hand of his
prostrate foe, and tied his arms firmly with

the whip-lash. Then he proceeded, leading his horse, to the other robber, whom he pulled over so as to examine his face, and with the cool remark of " Dead as a her-ring ! I thowt how it 'ud be wi' him : a whipstock 's a dangerous thing," went on to look at Mr. Oliphant.

The latter was very faint with loss of blood, and much battered besides with the blows he had received. But he was con-scious, and feebly muttered his thanks.

" I did not deserve this from you, Mr. Wideawake," he added courteously.

" Hod yer noise, now," said the farmer, good-naturedly ; " I'd hev done twice as mich for ony stranger, an' I'se reght glad I've been able to help ye, just to show ye 'at I bear ye na malice. But ye're bleed-ing fearfully. I mun manish to tee yer showder up somehow, an' then we'll carry ye down to t' Hall. It's rayther nearer nor Sandy Topping, an' it's down-hill. Yan on 'em's dead, an' I've gitten t'other fast. I'll mak him help to carry ye, the scamp; he sall sweat to-neght for this job."

Accordingly, first tying up Mr. Oliphant's shoulder with a handkerchief, Dick turned his horse loose into a field, and lifting a gate off its hinges, covered it with his own coat. Laying the old man on this rude litter, he then went and kicked up his prisoner, first seeing that his hands were tied firmly, but not so close as to prevent his carrying his full share of the gate.

"Now then, ye scoundrel," said Dick, putting his fist menacingly close to the other's face, "ye and I hev to carry him down to t' village; an' if I find ye don't do it as deftly as if ye wor carrying a basket o' new-laid eggs, or if ye trip, or thraw him down, or do ought 'at's unmannerly, I'll screw yer neck for ye at yance. I willn't mak ony banes about it, an' sae ye knaw. Now, tak hod; t' feet 'll be t' heavier, sae ye sall hev 'em."

As the road was down-hill, they were not long in carrying Jabez to the village, Dick enjoying amazingly his task of negro driving, and thundering in no measured accents every other minute at his poor slave in front. At the village four men were quickly procured to carry Mr. Oliphant forward to the Hall, whither, at his special request, both Dick and the prisoner accompanied him, while others ran for a constable and a surgeon.

When the latter came he pronounced the wounds not immediately dangerous, but declined to venture on any prophecy as to their result. He thought that if Mr. Oliphant had been a strong young man his recovery would have been almost a cer-

tainty, but there was no saying how an old
man would bear the shock. It was found
that the knife had passed completely
through the upper part of the arm, and
had then glanced upwards from one of the
ribs, and inflicted an ugly gash in the
shoulder. The very fury of the scoundrel
had thus defeated his purpose, for he had
not observed the old man's arm, which lay
on the chest and protected it.

"You will come and see me in the morning, Richard?" said Mr. Oliphant, as they
carried him to his room. "You are a fine
fellow, and perhaps I have not treated you
well : but I do not think I shall get over
this ; so you will come and see me?"

"Oh, ay ; I'll come an' see ye, Mr. Oliphant, if ye like ; an', bless ye, ye'll live
to larn some mair Craven dialect yet."

Jabez, after being swathed in bandages,
passed a tolerable night, but was still very

weak in the morning, when Dick and the surgeon came again to see him. Meanwhile, they had fetched the dead man down to one of the village inns, and had found him a stranger. But, when they washed the face of the other man, some one remembered him as the Anthony Bowskill whom Mr. Oliphant, years before, had caught in the act of killing a hare. The prisoner, however, remained obstinately silent, except once, when he said, sullenly nodding towards Mr. Oliphant's room,— " Let me speak to him, an' I'll answer aw he wants to larn, an' mebbe mair."

Now Mrs. Hardacre had told Mr. Oliphant during the night both Bowskill's name and the remark he had made, and Jabez was strangely anxious to talk with him. The surgeon, fearing excitement, was sorry the prisoner had ever been spoken of in his patient's hearing ; but when he understood that Mr. Oliphant had rambled a little, and often mentioned Bowskill, he thought it would be safer to allow the interview to take place.

"Thank you, sir," said Jabez, when the surgeon signified his consent; "it matters little whether I live or die; but I think I shall be easier when I have seen him."

Bowskill, therefore, was brought into the room, and placed in a chair near Mr. Oliphant. He was strongly handcuffed, and a constable and Dick kept a hand on him, one on each side, lest he should attempt further mischief.

"I understand you are Bowskill," said the old man to him faintly, and with frequent pauses, "and that you have said you would tell me why you made this dreadful attempt on my life."

"Well, can't ye guess?" asked the prisoner sullenly.

" No ; was it money ?"

" Nay, it wasn't money ; he 'at's dead did it for yer money, but I did it for spite ; an' I'se nobbut sorry we didn't manish it."

" Spite ! I have done you no wrong."

" Hevn't ye ?" said the other, contemptuously. " Ye grand folk think ye can tell ony lies, even when ye're deeing. I'se glad to see ye look sa death-like."

" Why are you so glad ?"

" Mebbe ye'll be saying it warn't yersel 'at drave me to bad ways first ? It wor ye, an' ye knaw it, 'at stopped wer wark at t' limekilns, for some o' yer new-fangled notions. I wor a workman there, an' I caw onybody to witness I wor as dacent a hand, barrin' a sup o' drink now an' then, as there wor about t' spot. I'd a wife an' fower childer to keep, an' I did it wi'out axing t' parish or onybody to help me."

" Is that true, Richard ?" asked Jabez.

"Ay, ay, I believe it is, sae far," answered the farmer; "he wor a gradely lad then."

"Well, ye stopped wer wark, but ye took care to give us nane i' its place. Ye happen fancy poor folk can live on air for a month or two, but ye're mistakken. I couldn't bear to see t' wife and childer clemmed, sae I took to catching a hare now an' then; an' nae girt harm in it auther, say I."

"It was against the law," said Mr. Oliphant, feebly.

"Ay, sae ye said that day ye cotched me," answered Bowskill, "but belly-law 's stronger than Lunnon-law. Howiver, ye seed me; an' then, spite of aw I could say, an' aw Miss Oliphant could say, ye gev me three months at Wakefield. But ye niver towd t' bench 'at it wor ye 'at hed driven me auther to poach or starve." As Mr. Oliphant remained silent, he continued :

"Well, that Wakefield wor t' ruination
o' me. I gat acquainted wi' Tom Riley (him
'at's dead) an' aw maks of bad characters.
When t' three months wor up I com back
to Reinsber, as if aw wor reght, but they'd
cropt my hair, an' iverybody as good as
cried 'Jail-bird' o' me. Sae t' wife thowt
we'd better move to where we warn't knawn;
an' we went to Accrington an' aw ower.
But it wor all'ays coming out 'at I'd been
i' t' House, an' then I gat turned off time
efter time, till I wor mad at iverybody an'
iverything, and ye maist of aw, acos ye wor
t' cause on it. Then I wor all'ays meeting
wi' Tom or some on 'em, an' at last yan
day, when I'd hed nae wark for a month, I
went wi' 'em an' began stealing. An' then
I persuaded Tom to come here ; an' we sud
ha' sattled ye, an' nae mistak, if Mr. Wideawake here hed bin a minute later, as I wish
he hed."

"Well, I am very truly sorry if I have been the cause, however innocently, of your ruin," said Jabez, sighing.

"Aa, what's t' good o' being sorry when I've gitten these things on?" (rattling the handcuffs). "We'd bin lying i' wait for ye near a week i' t' cave yonder, an' I engaged to Tom 'at, if he helped me i' this job, I'd help him to rob t' Grange at Stainton, or do ought 'at iver he liked. Ye may do what ye please wi' me now; I've said my say, an' I don't care: but it caps me 'at ye caw yersel a good man when wi' aw yer trials at makking folk vartuous ye end by makking 'em sa bad."

The prisoner sat sulkily back in his chair, after firing off this last sneer; but the surgeon, who had kept his hand on Mr. Oliphant's pulse, and now found it fluttering violently, signed to the constable to remove the man.

When Bowskill was out of the room, Mr. Oliphant said, in a low moaning voice, " I am glad I saw him ; but it is very sad, it kills me to see how unfortunate, as he says, all my efforts to do good have been. A fatality, which I cannot understand, has attended them all. Well, it is the weakness of dotage perhaps, but I must not do him any more harm, if I can help it." And though Dick whispered what consolation he could, Jabez continued moody and in low spirits for many days.

But, a short time afterwards, he got Doolittle to accompany his prisoner to Liverpool, and there see him, with his wife and family, on board a vessel bound for the United States, Mr. Oliphant paying the passage money. Tommy had also a hundred pounds with him, which he was to slip into Bowskill's hand as the last boat left the ship, and when it was quite certain therefore that he could not get back to England. All this Tommy did very faithfully, though he knew it was at some risk from the law, if Mr. Oliphant should die of his wounds ; but he yielded to the request of the poor old man, who declared that he should not rest in his grave if some reparation were not made for the ruin which he now accused himself of having brought on Bowskill. He desired, too, that if he died no proceedings should be taken against any one.

Then for many weeks Jabez Oliphant flickered between life and death, and Wide-awake, Doolittle, and Truman often visited him, especially the first, who seemed to be the most welcome of the three, probably from a natural feeling of gratitude on Mr. Oliphant's part to the man who had saved his life.

CHAPTER IV.

SINCE a marriage which was what the world would consider highly imprudent, Frank and Kate Holden had lived in London. They had only one or two hundred pounds in hand, and being too proud to trouble their friends, they suffered much, and had drained the cup of poverty almost to the dregs. Frank's pictures—perhaps he always rated them too high—had been rejected at the Academy, and the dealers became loth to buy his sketches, while Kate, who had tried to eke out their scanty means by teaching pupils, had been curtly dismissed, for some cause or other, by the

16—2

vulgar woman who did her the honour, as she thought, of employing her. Thus, after great privations, they had sunk far in the social scale, and—I should tremble for my hero and heroine if I wrote for snobs— Frank had at last been forced to return to his old trade of compositor, to keep themselves and their two children alive.

Still their love had never failed them. Never once had either of them, in their deepest poverty or suffering, wished the past undone. They had at all events tasted, what they would not have tasted otherwise, the supreme happiness of earth —that of mutual love. Frank's buoyant nature and good temper, therefore, with Kate's high spirit and devotion, carried them successfully through all their trials.

Fortune, they say, gets tired of striking those who smile at her knocks. It seemed so with our friends; for, during the summer that preceded the murderous attack on Mr. Oliphant, their prospects brightened considerably. An eccentric old connoisseur, named Dalton, seemed at last to have found out Frank's merits, for he insisted on giving the artist five guineas as the real value of a water-colour which had long been offered in some dealer's window for two.

So struck too was Mr. Dalton with our hero's talents, that he not only offered him other commissions, but wished him to give lessons in painting to his son, at a liberal salary. Thus Frank, though he would not abandon his printing, seemed at last on the road to fortune, and had many a good-humoured laugh against Kate, telling her that he, at any rate, had not to seek pupils over half London ; they came to him before he wanted them.

One afternoon, two or three days before

Christmas-day, whom should Frank see in the Strand, close to his present residence, but the last person he ever expected to meet in London, honest Dick Wideawake? The colossal farmer was strolling leisurely along, overtopping the crowd by head and shoulders and making it give way to his huge bulk, after the fashion of a ninety-gun ship swaggering through a fleet of small craft. The cockneys were turning round to look at him, for there was no mistake about the broad shoulders, rosy face and good-humoured strut being very fresh indeed from the country; even if there had not been the big knob-stick and unfashionable brown shooting-coat, and if Dick had not stared at all the shop-windows and everything in open-mouthed wonder. Great were the surprise and pleasure expressed on both sides when the dalesman and artist encountered each other.

"Why, Dick, who in the world would have thought of seeing you in town!" cried Holden.

"What, is it raelly ye, Mr. Holden! Nay, but this caps ought. Talk o' coming across a needle i' a bottle o' hay! Well, and how are ye? an' how's Mrs. Holden? an' whar hev ye bin these fower years?"

"Nay, I cannot answer all those questions," Holden replied laughing, "without you'll come in and have some tea with us. I live close by."

"Well, raelly; how extraordinary, now, isn't it, 'at I sud just leght on yower street! But I'll come in wi' as mich pleasure as I'd bury a rich cousin 'at I wor heir to, an' that 'ud be considerable."

Dick was too much one of nature's gentlemen even to appear to notice the poverty in which he found his friends; and Mrs. Holden was very glad both to see him, and to hear his news of Reinsber, from which place she had not received the slightest intelligence for more than two years. She was deeply affected when she heard of the recent attempt on her uncle's life, and of the precarious condition in which he was then lying.

"How I wish I could have been there to nurse him!" she exclaimed; "but you know it is impossible, after what he said. Still, to think of his lying there ill, as lonely as you say he is, and with nobody but servants to nurse him—dear, dear uncle! I *must* write to him, Frank, to say how sorry I am that he is ill."

"I think you ought, dear," said Frank. "Kate has written to him twice before, Dick, to tell him of our marriage, and of the birth of little Jabez here—we called the baby after him, though he doesn't know that; but he never answered either letter, and of course we don't like to write often, lest he should think we are trying to spunge on him."

" No, no, ye couldn't. He's as hard as a bull's horn, an' ye munnot look for ought frae him i' my opinion : I sudn't wonder, if he deed to-morn, he wadn't leave ye a farden piece."

" We do not want him to leave us anything, Mr. Wideawake," said Kate, rather proudly, " and we don't expect a farthing —it is not that. But you have not told us what has brought you to London."

" Brass, brass, to be sure, as usual. I com up wi' some tits to sell amang t' Cockneys ; for, says I to mysel, they're reckoned a sharp set, an' I sud like to hev a bit o' trade wi' 'em for yance, just for t' credit o' Yorkshire, like. Aa, but I'll tell ye what, Mr. Holden" (dropping his voice to a confidential half-whisper), " they're a soft lot :—their brains want a summer-run badly."

"Ha, you have had some good dealing with them, then, Dick?"

"I niver med as mich brass i' t' time i' aw my life, niver. It wor fair like coining. What, they'll buy ought! I varily believe if I'd browt up t' owd parson's mare 'at hed three game legs an' yan wooden 'un, they'd ha bowt her."

Holden reminded him that horses necessarily fetch better prices in London than in Yorkshire; but the farmer persisted in giving all the credit of his bargains to his own superior acuteness.

"And what do you think of London itself?" asked Kate.

"Well, I'se fair capped wi' it, I mun say that," answered the Yorkshireman, reluctantly. "Sich miles on miles o' streets an' grand houses, 'at yan wad think aw mankind hed done nought sin' Adam but build 'em. Dal it, I did a thing amang 'em I niver did afore—I lost mysel bodily yan day, I did, indeed" (a faint blush overspread Dick's cheeks at the remembrance of this disgrace), "an' I've crossed Stainton Moor mony a time i' a fog as straight as a craw flies. I gat quite maddled, like, an' when I fand mysel, I wor three mile frae my lodgings, an' ganging reght away frae 'em. I wadn't like to tell that to ivery body, but I don't mind ye, Mrs. Holden. Ay, ay, it's a grand place enough, an' I willn't say but I'se surprised at it—happen nigh as mich as a Londoner wad be if he wor clapped down at t' foot o' Penyghent when he'd niver seen a hill afore. But efter aw, ye see London's nobbut *made,* an' naebody could mak Penyghent—we bang 'em there, ye knaw."

"But which do you think the grandest

sight of all you have seen; the crowd, or the shops, or the public buildings?" asked Kate, considerably amused.

"Well, I don't think sa mich o' t' folk, as I teld ye, Mrs. Holden, though they do swarm like maggots i' a cheese; but then they're awmost as white an' as lile. An' then as to t' shop-windows, they're varra grand, na doubt, but it seems to me just sae mich money an' trouble thrawn away: ye can git aw ye want at lile Tommy Doolittle's, an' ye couldn't possibly git mair, ye knaw, if he wor to prop up hauf his house wi' plate-glass, as they do here. Nay, t' strangest seght I've seen wor a chap wi'out arms, 'at wor writing wi' his toes for hawpennies. My eyes, but that wor a capper!"

"O Mr. Wideawake!" laughed Kate; "but surely you have not seen Westminster Abbey, or the Houses of Parliament, or St. Paul's?"

"Ay, but I hev; an' when I wor moping about i' t' Abbey, there wor a chap comes up to me, an' says he, 'Well, sir, you have nothing as grand as this with you, I fancy.' 'Hevn't we?' says I, as scornful as I could; 'why, it's just nought at aw—yan 'ud put six like this inside York Minster as easy as ye'd set six eggs under an owd hen, an' ye'd hev room for a dozen o' yer biggest London churches i' t' spaces atween 'em :'— weel, weel, I knaw, Mrs. Holden, it warn't quite exactly correct, but then I wor bound to bounce a bit for t' honour o' t' owd county, warn't I, now? An' as it happened, he hedn't been to York, so ye see it wor aw as reght as a trivet. 'Why,' says I, 'we've a hoil i' Yorkshire just at my back-door'—Guzzle Pot, ye knaw, Mr. Holden; now, ye can testify to that, yersel —''at 'ud hod this thing o' yowers, an' think nought about it; an' t' beck running in 'ud fill it with watter i' ten minutes, as easy as it 'ud fill a mug pot.' 'But don't you think the monuments to all these great men very fine?' says he. 'Ay,' says I, 'ye've buried 'em weel, I grant, but then we bred 'em, ye knaw?' Sae wi' that off he went like a hare wi' a shot i' its lug."

Frank was curious to know whether the big horse-jobber, who seemed such a likely prey, had escaped the London pickpockets.

"Pickpockets! Nay, I nobbut met wi' yan o' them gentry. Ye see I'se i' t' habit o' ganging about to fairs sae mich 'at, though I look careless about my pockets, I isn't: I can tell i' a crack if onybody touches 'em."

"But I hope you did not lose much by the one thief you did come across," said Frank.

"I lost nought at all. I wor standing watching a chap i' Holburn 'at wor trying to sell sovereigns at a penny a piece for a

wager, an' there wor a biggish crowd about.
Well, I felt a lile leght hand stealing
deftly into my coat-pocket; sae I let t' hand
git weel in, an' then I grabbed hod on it.
He wor a pale wizened chap of about five-
an'-twenty: aa, how he did tremmle when
I cotched him!"

"And what did you do to him? Did
you give him into custody?" asked
Kate.

"Nay, I thowt it wor nae good bothering
wi' him, sa I just chucked him into a muck-
cart 'at happened to be passing handy. He
wor a seght when he com' up again an' t'
folk did laugh, I can tell ye. That wor t'
first day I wor here, an' I've niver bin
troubled wi' ony pickpockets sin'."

"With very good reason, I think," cried
Holden laughing: "Your reformatory was
of a new kind, Dick."

"Ay, but t' varra same day I wor passing

down a side street, when there wor a shabby chap com up to me an' axed me t' way to t' Tower. 'I'se a stranger here, sir,' says I. 'Indeed!' says he; 'perhaps you are fresh from the country like myself? I'm quite delighted to meet with any one that is not a cockney: do come and have a glass of something with me.' *Ye* fra t' country! thinks I, noticing t' cut of his jib; now what divilment are ye efter, young man? Begow, but I'll see t' boddom o' this; an' if ye can do Dick Wideawake ye're welcome to aw ye git frae him. But I pretended to be quite simple, like, an' said I'd gang wi' him wi' aw t' pleasure i' life. Sa then he tuk me into a parlour i' a public-house, whar was another chip o' t' same block, as I seed by their looks 'at they knew each other, though they didn't speak."

"These rogues generally work in pairs, I believe," said Holden.

"Sae when we'd gitten wer liquor, we talked on a bit, an' then yan on 'em browt out a pack o' cards an' wanted me to layke wi' 'em. Ho, ho, thinks I, that's it, is it? Ye want some o' my brass that way, do ye? 'Nay,' says I to 'em, 'I'se varra sorry, I dunnot play cards.' 'Well, do you play skittles, then?' says t' other; 'there's a ground at t' back.' 'I mak naa doubt on't,' says I; 'but I cannot play.' Well, they kept on bothering me to layke at some'at, sa thinks I, I'll just teach ye a lesson, young men, for t' futur. Then I says to 'em quite simply, 'Nay, t' only game 'at I knaw ought about is draughts, an' I sudn't hev minded an odd game at that; but t' warst on't is I git sae excited at it, an' I've a plaguy lot o' money about me: Dal it,' says I, 'I sud happen git agate betting an' loss it aw.' Aa but didn't their eyes glisk when I teld 'em o' t' brass! 'Oh no !' says yan on 'em, winking to t' other, ' I never gamble : but do let us have a game at draughts.' Sa he ordered in a draught-board an' set t' men, as girt as a kitten ower its first mouse ; an' we sattled 'at t' first ame wor to be for a shilling a side. Well, he hedn't med ten moves afore I seed I could lick his heead off—I'se a dab hand at t' game, Mrs. Holden, though I say it my-sel."

"I have always heard you spoken of as the very best player about Reinsber," said Kate.

" At any rate there isn't yan 'at can beat me, an' we play a deal. Howiver, I let him win t' first game as it wor nobbut for a shil-ling, an' then, thinking he could lick me easy, he proposed we sud play t' next game for a pound a side. ' Agreed,' says I. Sae there wor an honest-looking chap 'at hed just come in for a glass of ale, an' we gat him to hod t' stakes : they wanted to give

'em to t' waiter, but I wadn't do that.
Well, I won t' game, but I did it sae 'at he
thowt it wor bungler's luck; an' he proposed,
aw' i' a huff, 'at we sud hev another for five
pund a side. 'Down wi' yer brass, then,'
says I, 'only we'll hev gowd not notes,' for
I wor flaid o' flash notes, ye see. To mak
up t' five pund, they'd to help yan another
out, an' I don't believe they'd hauf-a-crown
left atween 'em when they'd staked. Sae
that game, I just shawed him what I could
do; I *two'd* him an' *three'd* him to a bonny
tune, I can tell ye. An' just at t' last he
began shuffling about trying to upset t'
board."

"It was a wonder he did not," said
Frank.

"Oh, but I says to him, 'Tak care what
ye're about, maister; I'se a bit hasty, an'
I've knawn when I've banged a fellow's
baan-cart black an' blue for spilling t' board

when he wor licked.’   I spak quite soft but I looked hazle-oil, I mak naa doubt, an’ they durstn’t do it.   Sae I won t’ brass; an’ then he wanted me to layke at cards for ten pund; but I tuk my hat an’ teld ’em I wad be ganging, for I thowt they wor near about cleared out.   ‘Thank ye,’ says I, ‘for yer drink an’ yer money baith, gentlemen; an’ t’ next time ye meet a countryman i’ Lunnon, ax him first thing if he’s a York-shireman, afore ye bring him in.’   They did look black, aw except t’ stakeholder; an’ I gev him ten shilling when I com away.”

Thus with Dick’s long-winded narratives and with chat of various kinds they whiled away the evening not unpleasantly.   In the course of it, the farmer said he had a com-mission from his wife to Mrs. Holden if he did happen to see her; and he was delighted to have the chance, so very unexpectedly, of executing it.

" And what is it, Mr. Wideawake ?" asked Kate.

" Well, we just want ye an' Mr. Holden an' t' babby to come down an' spend yer Christmas holidays wi' us at Sandy Topping. Now, ye yance promised to come ; an' I expect ye will. A bit o' country air 'll do ye aw a power o' good, an' I can't say 'at ye're looking exactly weel, Mrs. Holden. An' then, ye see, ye'll be able to hear how yer uncle gangs on."

In fine Dick pressed them so hard, and the proposal was so agreeable to them, that at last they consented, and in high spirits set out with the hospitable farmer for Sandy Topping early on Christmas-eve.

CHAPTER V.

A MERRY CHRISTMAS.

IT was a long day's journey by rail from London to Stainton ; for our travellers, from motives of economy, started by the government train at seven. The Holdens had not been out of town since their wedding trip, and their pleasure at seeing the country once more, even in winter and from the windows of a third-class railway-carriage, was great. Dick's lively sallies, too, helped to pass the day very agreeably; but towards the end of it Kate, who had been unwell, became so much tired, that though she had been anticipating the first sight of Reinsber with a good deal of pleasure, she was no sooner transferred to the fly, which the farmer engaged at Stainton railway station to carry them to Sandy Topping, than she fell fast asleep. It was seven o'clock at night, however, and very dark, so that she could have seen but little of the village even if she had kept awake.

"This is a dreadful extravagance for you, Dick," said Holden, meaning the fly.

"Oh, I med sa mich brass up yonder, 'at I can afford to spend a bit of it on owd friends like ye," answered Dick. "Are ye sure ye've gitten aw yer luggage, now?"

"The 'all' is easily looked after; but there it is, baby and all. Kate is asleep; so I'll just take him from her."

"Do; an' we'd best not talk till we git hame: we sall nobbut wakken her, poor thing. It's a lang journey for yan 'at isn't strong."

The conveyance rattled on for half-an-hour, till the scattered lights on each side apprised them that they were passing through Reinsber ; then all grew darkness again.

"Don't you think we are a long time in coming to the Brow, Dick ?" said Holden, whispering for fear of disturbing Kate.

"Whisht ! we'se wakken her. But t' boddom o' t' hill is a good way frae t' village : ye don't recollect it reght, Mr. Howden."

By-and-bye the fly stopped, and the door was thrown open with a bang ; and Kate, still only half awake, and scarcely knowing where she was, was handed out and stood in a blaze of light from the open door before her. The bright light, the crowd of servants waiting on the steps, the size of the house and doorway—all this startled her, for it was not what she expected at Sandy Topping, nor did the place look at all like the farmer's comfortable but rough abode.

She gave one fluttered glance round to

see where she was, and instantly recognised the stately building with its mighty sycamores, as the dear old Hall where she had spent some pleasant years in that far-off time of her girlhood, and from which she had been cast adrift so unceremoniously.

"Mr. Wideawake, how durst you?" she asked indignantly, and (as the farmer only answered with one of his jolly laughs) would have stepped back instantly into the fly; but she felt some one's arms round her, detaining her, and though dizzy with excitement, she heard the words, in feeble tones, but how familiar!—"Nay, dearest Kate, it was not Mr. Wideawake's doing, it was mine. I sent for you, and will you not forgive me and stay?" Then she turned giddily and saw that it was indeed her uncle—pale, feeble, tottering, a wreck of a man—but her uncle still, and smiling on her!

With a faint cry of surprise and joy, she threw herself in his arms, weeping and without a word. Then she kissed him a dozen times delightedly, and suffered herself to be led into the house by the old man, who whispered excitedly to the others : " Look after these gentlemen, please, Mrs. Hardacre ; Mrs. Holden and I will go to the drawing-room and have a quiet talk first—give us a few minutes, Mr. Holden— just a few minutes, if you please." Then he walked into the house, with a slow, faltering step, keeping fast hold of Kate, who soon found that her support was necessary to him, for he had exerted himself greatly to leave his room at all.

The old man tottered, with her help, to the well-pillowed sofa he had quitted when he heard the sound of the wheels ; and Kate, with a woman's instinct, quickly beat up the pillows and arranged them, before he lay down. Then she threw her bonnet and shawl hastily on the table and sat down beside him, looking at his face and resting her own on the arm of the sofa, while he took her hand in both his, pale and shaking as they were. So they sat looking at each other for a moment or two, both of them with tears in their eyes, but wonderful satisfaction in their breasts.

"These pillows are easier already, dear," said Mr. Oliphant, with a faint pleased laugh. "But I did not send for you for that. I know now that I did you wrong."

"Dearest uncle," said Kate, softly stealing her arm round his neck and kissing him again fondly, "do not speak of it again."

"I must, Kate : I should like to talk it over first thing, and have done with it. But I think you'll forgive me, as you have taken off your bonnet. That looks like stopping, eh ?"

"I have nothing to forgive ; you were

always only too kind to me, dear uncle. And I'll stay always, if you ask me."

"That is all right, then ; and I do ask you."

"But did you really arrange beforehand that we should come here, uncle?" asked Kate, still wrapped in wonder at the whole affair, and at her mistaken estimate of his obstinacy, which, she had often told Frank, would last.

"Yes, it was all my doing, Kate. I arranged everything with Wideawake, and sent him up to town with some horses for a pretext ; he was to meet Frank accidentally, to get you all to come down to Sandy Topping, and then drive you here, without your knowing where you were till I had you safe. And here you are !"

"I would have come to you at once, uncle, from the end of the earth, if I had known you wished it."

"Ay ; but as we knew you had a good

deal of spirit, we thought you might flatly decline to come at all after what had happened."

"Nothing ever happened that could have made me behave so badly as that."

"Well, I did not know. There was what I said to you about your looking after my money, you see," the old man replied in a penitent voice. "But believe me, Kate, I was so angry at the time that I did not even remember I had used the words at all, till Wideawake reminded me of them since I have been ill."

"Dear uncle, it is enough that you did not mean what you said."

"It was very wrong to say so, and very unjust to you. You always loved me for myself alone, and few have done that. Then, I never knew till lately from Wideawake how nearly I caused your death that terrible night, when I turned you out, so unmercifully: and the thought of this, too, was so dreadful to myself, that I did not know whether you could forgive me."

Kate's answer was a tear and another kiss. Then after a pause, she said: "But have you forgiven me, dear uncle, for not agreeing to your wishes about Lord Stainmore? Indeed, indeed, I was very sorry I could not do it."

"Nay, Kate; I fear my obstinacy about that matter is another count in the indictment against me. I have something to say about Lord Stainmore presently."

"But why did you not send for me long since, uncle? Though indeed I have been the worse of the two in allowing a silly indignation at a word or two to keep me from the best friend I ever had; and I ought to have known that you might have forgotten the words. As to my little night adventure at Reinsber, why, you know, that was entirely my own fault. You had a perfect right to send me away if you liked, and I ought to have waited for a cab or something, and not have gone off in the huff. Yes, I ought to have come back long since, and it is you who must forgive *me*."

The old man blushed a little, and said nervously: "Nay, Kate; it is better to make a clean breast of it, and I must say— of course I feel how wrong it is now—but I fear if you had come back, except very recently, I should have given you a sorry welcome."

"The welcome is all the dearer for being long deferred, uncle."

"You are very kind, Kate. But really, till about six months ago I was as angry at you as ever. I was very lonely and miser- able—you have heard of my disputes with the other people ?—but I could not forgive you ; for I thought you ought to have re- turned to me, I not remembering my own words, you know.   Then I began to soften just a little towards you, when I recollected, as I did day by day, how kind and affectionate you had always been to me, and how different from all the rest of the hard world : so by degrees I came to think that it was not right to let you and Mr. Holden starve."

"I think we almost deserved it, after all."

" Nay, nay.   But, as I say, till about July, I was so hardened against you that I did not care to know where you were, or what you were doing.   In fact, I only heard of you occasionally through Lord Stainmore, who, of course, told me only what prejudiced me still farther against you—for instance, that you were getting into debt."

" That was a base calumny, uncle," said Kate, with some spirit.   " If we had got into debt we should not have suffered as we did."

"Of course, I know that, now, Kate," answered her uncle. "But I think I was rather infatuated with that young man. Would you believe it?—I had really made my will in his favour, and left you nothing."

"Well, uncle, and why not?" said Kate, meeting her uncle's eye with a full unshrinking look. "Except that Lord Stainmore is in my opinion a very bad man, I know no reason whatever why you should not leave your money to him or any one else you like. If I stay with you, dear uncle, as you wish, it must be on the full understanding that I do not expect a farthing piece from you, unless you choose to give it."

"Dear Kate, you must really forget those unhappy words of mine: I know without that look how unjust they were. But we will talk about money by and by. Lord Stainmore, at any rate, shall not have any of mine," added Jabez, with sudden and sharp dignity : "he is, as you say, a very bad man, and perhaps the most crotchety man I ever met."

" O uncle, I am very glad you have found him out ; but how did this happen ?"

"Well, he paid me a visit here last spring," replied Jabez, hesitating a little, as if he wished to avoid the subject; " and he then advanced such opinions, so untenable, so plainly erroneous, so pernicious, in one word, that—that in fact I thought it only right afterwards to make some further inquiries, through my solicitor in London, into the antecedents of the man to whom I proposed to leave the bulk of my fortune. Those inquiries satisfied me that Mr. Holden and yourself had been very correctly informed about him."

Her uncle evidently did not wish to say anything more about his quarrel with the viscount than he could help, and Kate did not press him on the subject. As the reader, however, may be more curious than Mrs. Holden, he will perhaps like to hear a few particulars about the matter.

When Lord Stainmore visited the Hall, then, he found that the busy amiability of Mr. Oliphant's disposition, which was so unhappily restricted at home, had made outlets for itself at such a distance from the Reinsber carles, that one would have thought it could hardly be interfered with again. He had become deeply interested in astronomy, and more especially in the important, but now trite, question whether Venus and the other planets are inhabited. He stoutly maintained to the viscount that this was not only possible but certain, basing his assertion mainly on the premisses that, "God being a benignant ruler, it was inconsistent alike with His love and the admitted principles of good government, divine or human, to leave so large a portion of the universe idle and untenanted, when it might be filled with beings, each of them doing his appointed work in the great commonwealth of spheres, and each of them, by his own happiness, adding to the general sum of felicity which an all-benevolent Being would necessarily make as large as possible." Of secondary arguments, too, Mr. Oliphant had so many in support of his theory, that the only additional proof which seemed wanting to absolute demonstration was the production of some actual inhabitant of another planet.

Lord Stainmore, however, either tired of constant acquiescence, bored with the subject, or, more likely still, from a love of fun and a wish to enliven the dulness of the Hall by poking up the old man's temper, had warmly espoused the opposite side of the question. No doubt, had he been aware of the honour and profit intended him in Mr. Oliphant's will, he would have been more cautious ; but even men of the world cannot know everything, and, as Jabez had kept the disposition of his property a profound secret, the viscount did not dream that there was anything to be gained, now Kate was gone, by keeping on good terms with Mr. Oliphant.

For once, therefore, his lordship spoke out like a man, took a firm stand on mother-earth, and declined to concede a single inhabitant, or even the most infinitesimal possibility of one, to all the members of the solar system combined, and expressed it as his own decided opinion that the real God of the universe was " an embodiment of enlightened selfishness, and, like the god of the Epicureans, much too wise to trouble Himself at all, either for the sake of good

government or anything else, about the
tiresome doings or silly sayings, the sentimental happiness or sententious misery, of
a paltry pack of little vermin like ourselves." As Lord Stainmore phrased it,
with some irreverence, "The Almighty
might be a philosopher, but certainly was
not a philanthropist."

Thus pressed by argument and occasionally assailed even with a little ridicule, the
old man answered with temper, and, the
influence of chilling Saturn predominating,
or the fierier sphere of Mars being in the as-
cendant, quarrelled with the viscount out-
right. Offended, too, at the gross blasphemy
which could deny that the Almighty was,
like Jabez himself, an ideal ruler and a philanthropist, and still more deeply wounded,
perhaps, by an atrocious assertion of Lord
Stainmore's, viz., that he could see absolutely
nothing in the other's arguments, Mr. Oli-

phant felt it his duty, as he told Kate, to investigate his lordship's previous history, and finally burnt the will he had made in his favour. So Lord Stainmore, for the sake of a joke on the nebulæ, unconsciously lost a good many acres on terra firma, and the quarrel had this good result, that it made the old man review his own conduct to Kate, and predisposed him to a reconciliation.

"About last July, then," continued Mr. Oliphant to Kate, "I began to think that, after all, I would make you a small allowance indirectly, without your knowing from whom it came—just to keep you from starving. So I wrote to an old friend of mine in the city, a merchant called Dalton, whom I could trust——"

"Dalton!" exclaimed Kate, in surprise, a new light dawning on her.

"Mr. Dalton," answered Jabez, with a

pleased chuckle. "You seem to have heard the name before. Mr. Dalton, however, was rather negligent about my commission at first, and it was not till I urged him strongly two or three months afterwards, that he tried to find you out in earnest. This, however, was so difficult, he wrote me, that he despaired of success till he accidentally discovered some of Mr. Holden's paintings which were exposed for sale at a picture-dealer's. And even then the dealer told him that no address was left with them, as Mr. Holden always called in person."

"We were so poor, you know, we did not wish to have persons coming to our lodgings."

"Very natural; only it was a pity in this case, and caused you, I fear, some suffering which might have been avoided. Well, Mr. Dalton paid Frank better for his paintings, and gave him some fresh commissions—of course for me. He also, at my request, allowed Frank to teach his son. You must forgive me this little bit of deception, Kate."

"Then after all, Mr. Dalton's purchases were not caused, as we thought, by appreciation of Frank's superior genius!" said Kate, rather piqued, but quite unable to resist a laugh. "But, dear uncle, we must not tell Frank this, if possible; it might pain him a little."

"Not one word about the matter from me, dear, though I can assure you the paintings are really well worth the money, and show remarkable talent—at least I am told so by good judges. You have reason to be proud of your husband, Kate."

"I am very proud of him," said Kate decisively, as if she would admit no scepticism on that point. "He is truly noble

and unselfish. I hope you will like him
thoroughly."

"You forget, Kate, that I know him
very well, and do like him so well already
that I have no doubt we shall get on admirably. To continue: It was after Mr.
Dalton met with you that my own adventure happened; and as Wideawake had
saved me, I naturally—from gratitude, and
perhaps a lingering fondness for him as a
friend of yours—asked him to come and see
me often. He did come, and he talked
very freely, I can assure you —with extreme
freedom," added Jabez, rather wincing at
the recollection.

"I hope he was not rude. But he is
very rough in his manner; it is all his
manner, I think."

"Nay, I deserved all he said. But we
had many interviews, and he did not spare
me. Still, whatever he said was a home-

thrust, for, as I say, he told me much about you that I did not know."

"We have discussed that before, dear uncle; do pass on to something else."

"Well, then there was poor Bowskill's case, the man who stabbed me; I found out that he was the very poacher I fined some years ago, and he accused me of being the cause of his ruin through my excessive strictness. So all these things together set me on a thorough review of my whole life at Reinsber, and I began to see how mistaken I had been in almost everything I had done."

"You never did anything except with the very best motives, and to make people good. Every one knows that."

"But how has it all turned out? There's the rub. Heaven knows I meant well, but I mistook the way—sadly, irretrievably, fatally. I might just as well

never have been born ; a sad thought for
an old man, Kate.   I took the wrong turning, and now it is too late to retrace my
steps, when death's hand is almost on me."

Kate had passed through many trials,
but never had she been more moved than
now ; she sprang up hastily, and kissed
him repeatedly before she could say, in a
faltering voice—

" Death's hand, dearest uncle !   Oh, not
so ; surely not so.   You shall not die if
the deepest love and the most devoted
attention on my part can save you.   You
will try to live for my sake, will you not,
dearest ?"

" Oh, I'll try, dear," said her uncle, play-
fully, returning her embrace : " and I must
say I feel wonderfully better already.   Till
to-night, you see, I did not much care
about living, for what had I, a poor lonely
old fellow, who had driven all my friends
from my side, to live for ?   But I am rather

tired, and I ought not to excite myself, the doctor tells me ; so, if I am to try to live, I think we will have Frank and Wideawake up, and then, if you will excuse me, I'll retire. Then, everything is to be between us for the future as if this dispute had never happened ?"

" Oh, yes."

" Well, I should like you to know—I think it best—that I have secured three thousand a year on you, in any case, and shall give Mr. Holden the papers to-morrow ; so that if ever I turn wicked again, you know—"

" Nay, uncle, you must not do this," said Kate, rather warmly.

But the old man insisted, and presently Frank and the honest farmer came in, much pleased at the reconciliation which had taken place. Soon afterwards Mr. Oliphant left them, after desiring Frank to be as much at home in the Hall as he was him-

self.   Dick, too, was anxious to be at
Sandy Topping ; but Frank and Kate had
a long chat before they retired, for she had
much to tell him, and had need of all her
powers of persuasion.

When he was informed of Mr. Oliphant's
intended munificence with respect to Kate,
and his wish that they should stay constantly at the Hall, the artist was disposed
to mount the high horse.

"I don't see why we should become
pensioners of his, Kate, when we are able
to keep ourselves.   Why should we be indebted to him ?   If he had wanted to help
us, he might have helped us before."

"Yes, dear, but he will not be happy unless we stay.   Besides, it will be much
pleasanter living here."

"Ah, the flesh-pots of Egypt !   I prefer
poverty and independence."

"But you would be able to give all your

time to art, and to get on at it so much better.   Now, do consent, Frank."

" I shall get on very well, you will see, as it is.   My wages as a compositor will keep us; and I think " (rather grandly) " the appreciation of a connoisseur like Dalton shows that my pictures cannot be so very bad after all.   It is not everybody that has five pounds given him for a painting which he is willing to sell for two. What are you laughing at, Kate ?   Is what I say true or not ?"

" Well, it is partly true, and partly not," replied Kate, who saw that if she would move her husband from his determination, she must play her best card ; " but—but— dear Frank, I hope you will not be vexed, as he only did it from motives of kindness —I find now it was my uncle who commissioned Mr. Dalton to buy your pictures for him, and to find you a pupil; so that

—whether we like it or not—we have taken money of his for some time."

Frank's face for a minute or two presented a somewhat ludicrous expression of fallen greatness.

"And so, it was not the merit of the things after all that sold them, you would say," he replied, rather angrily. Then, his ordinary good-nature returning, he burst into a laugh and exclaimed, "Well, it is certainly a good joke to find Dalton only Mr. Oliphant's agent; and I see I must be more cautious for the future about airing my artistic vanity. However, we have still the printing to fall back on, Kate. Your uncle did not graciously provide me with that too, I suppose?"

His wife saw that the fortress was carried, and that he was only resisting now for the purpose of yielding with a better grace.

" Yes, dear," she said, laughing and kissing him, " there is still the printing, and all your pupils besides, present and prospective. You have not to seek them over half London, you know—they come to you unasked—and they are always paying compliments to your talents !"

" Come, Kate, let us go to bed," replied the artist, taking up a candle. " I do think it is rather too bad that whenever I have a good bit of chaff against you, fortune always lets you turn the tables on me sooner or later."

" Then we stay here, Frank—that is settled ? Do let us, now."

" I surrender at discretion—making only one condition, that I never hear the name of that confounded fellow Dalton again— or—or in fact anything about art. I'm sick of it. Come along."

Then they retired, Kate having as usual

carried her point; but for many months Frank did not hear the last of his superior powers in the art of attracting pupils, or of that great genius which could raise the price of a picture from two guineas to five, through spontaneous admiration on the part of the purchaser.

CHAPTER VI.

AND A HAPPY NEW YEAR.

THE next morning—Christmas-day—Mr. Oliphant declared that he had passed an excellent night, and the doctor also thought him much better.

"Your coming, Mrs. Holden, has just supplied the fillip which was wanting to the system," said the man of drugs. "His wounds are healed, but he is so entirely prostrated that I was really very much alarmed about him, and should not have wondered to hear of his dropping off any day,—chiefly, I think, because he seemed to have no interest in anything. You have done wonders already, and I hope he will soon be out of my hands, if you can only amuse him."

Kate, of course, promised to do her best, and then, with Frank, went off to church, where her unexpected reappearance (for the probability of her return had been kept secret) caused great excitement among all her old friends at Reinsber.   After service she was almost mobbed by the congregation in the eagerness of their welcome; Truman, Fothergill, and Dora, Sir George and Harry Highside being among the first who came up to her.   The Christmas dinner afterwards was a very merry one, though there were only the Holdens and Mr. Oliphant present; but Kate and Frank, as they thought of that miserable Christmas night four years before, and their recent sufferings in London, had every reason to be contented with the turn things had taken, while the old man himself seemed to have lost all his hauteur, and was fairly beaming with happiness. In truth, his pride and imperiousness had been all along, in great measure, the result of habit. By nature he was kind and genial, but the exactitude required in business, and the necessity (as he conceived) of keeping a tight hand on the numerous persons in his employ in London, had engrafted on him an imperious bearing, which it took many hard shocks to remove.

As he continued to improve in health, that wily Kate planned a scheme for accomplishing what she had very much at heart, as likely to contribute more to his happiness than anything—a grand reconciliation, namely, between the carles and him. She soon ascertained that most of them pitied the old man now, and that there would be no obstacle on their side : but Jabez required cautious handling.

"Uncle," she said, "I am going to ask a favour; and I shall not think I am your own little niece again unless you grant it."

"And what is it, Kate? It must be something very preposterous if I do not," he answered.

"Well, you know Frank and I were married very quietly in London, and we had absolutely no wedding breakfast, or rejoicings over such a great event—as, of course, there ought to have been. Will you let us have them now? and I wish to ask all my friends, without exception."

"I shall be delighted; but whom would you ask?"

"Oh, numbers of people; first, everybody that was ever kind to us in London; and then all my friends from Reinsber, that is——"

"Well, Kate?" he said, still smiling.

She kissed him, and then went on boldly, "That is, dear uncle, *every*body in Reinsber,—men, women, and children; let us have them all, and give them a first-rate tea and supper on New Year's day. Poor things, you do not know how they'll enjoy the treat, or what a pleasure it will be to me. And let us ask Mr. Truman, Fothergill, and Dora, and, if you do not mind, Sir George and Mr. Hawtrey to dinner on the same day."

"They will never come, Kate," said Jabez, gravely.

"Oh yes, they will, as I shall manage it. Let me try, now."

"But you forget, dear, that at such a feast I should be eating humble-pie with a vengeance—not but that I deserve it, perhaps."

"What nonsense! They will be my visitors, not yours; and you need not have anything to do with them unless you like, uncle."

"Well, if you think so, do what you wish, Kate. And about myself, I cannot tell what I must do ; I will think it over."

So Kate wrote first to the few persons in London who had shown kindness to Frank or herself in their distress. Then she invited all the Reinsber carles, who received the news with delight, as she expected. She had a little more difficulty with one or two of the guests who were to come to dinner—Sir George especially, who had not yet forgot Mr. Oliphant's conduct to him. She got over all objections, however, by saying that the party was hers, and she had nothing to do with any old disputes. Thus, even the baronet, in his gallantry to the sex, was obliged to succumb, and consented to dine with her. With the parson, Hawtrey, and Fothergill, she had no trouble, as

all of them were rather amused than pro-
voked at what had happened, and were
quite willing to be reconciled to Mr. Oliphant or anybody.

Then during a few days every one at the
Hall was very busy, for about a couple of
hundred children were expected to tea, and
nearly the same number of grown-up people to supper, to say nothing of the more
elaborate repast in the dining-room. On
the last night in the year Jabez said to his
niece, " I think, Kate, after all, I shall make
my appearance to-morrow : it would look
better ; and besides, on thinking the thing
over, I do feel myself somewhat to blame
for a good deal of the unhappy wrangling
that has taken place, and feeling that, it
will be only right to say so—just a word
or two. Then we shall begin the new year
properly, shall we not ?" And Kate expressed much pleasure at his resolution.

When the first day of January arrived, great was the excitement among the young folks, for games had been provided for them on the lawn, and the Holdens, and even Mr. Oliphant, so far as his strength allowed, joined in football, blind-man's-buff, or some of the other good old English sports there going on during the afternoon. At four o'clock they mustered for tea, which was provided in the kitchen and another very large room. After the meal an immense Christmas tree was lighted up, and received with shouts of delight, more especially as, hanging on the branches, there were two or three gifts for each child that was present. When the little ones were dismissed, the tables were again spread for the older people with a right royal repast, Dick Wide-awake taking the head of one of the long tables, and Tommy Doolittle of the other ——though the worthy teetotaller was scandalised at the fact that every one was supplied with as much good ale as he wished.

The state dinner was also a success. Mr.
Oliphant, in a few courteous words of welcome and apology, told the guests severally
how glad he was to see them once more at
the Hall, and how sorry if he had given
them any just cause for staying away. Sir
George alone was rather surly, most of the
rest passing the matter off with a laugh and
a joke; but as the wine circulated, he too
became affable, and shook Mr. Oliphant's
hand cordially on leaving.

When supper was just over in the
kitchen, Jabez and Kate went in to see how
the carles were getting on with their meal,
and then he took the opportunity of delivering himself of his speech, which his
weakness probably made shorter than it
would otherwise have been. The men and
women were a good deal touched with pity

at his appearance, as he stood pale, bent, and emaciated, and supporting himself on a stick, at the end of one of the tables. When Dick, as president, had knocked loudly for silence, Mr. Oliphant said :

" I thought, my dear friends and neighbours, I should like to tell you how very glad I am to see you here once more. I fear you and I have misunderstood each other; and perhaps we have both been somewhat to blame, but certainly I myself most. But when I first came here, I had been accustomed to a different kind of life, and I fancy I thought myself a greater and a wiser man than I am." [An emphatic " No, no," from Tommy.] " However, I have learned at least two very valuable lessons. For as I come nearer the grave—and I am very near it now—the difference between one man and another seems to me less and less at every step I take ; and I find that if you did not care about doing some things that I wished, you have other counter-balancing virtues, such as a sterling independence, and sometimes a rough nobility of character which might put myself to the blush. Witness my friend Mr. Wideawake's conduct in saving me after I had been so hard on him. That was lesson the first. Then, again, I see that they who try to set the world to rights, as I did, often do more wrong than they set right ; that in fact the 'summum jus' is now, as of old, only another name for the 'summa injuria;' and that you may bend the bow of justice till it snaps, and hurts both yourself and every one about. I am rather tired and cannot say more, except to hope that we shall be good friends again, and to wish you all the happiest of New Years."

Dick Wideawake then jumped up, and after a brief prelude went on : " I couldn't

quite mak out that bit o’ French or some’at,
’at Mr. Oliphant used, nebbors ; but aw he
said just com to this, ’at he an’ we hev hed
a hardish feght for t’ maistery an’ he’s fand
out ’at brass—though it isn’t hauf a bad
thing i’ its way ” (Dick chinked some silver
lovingly in his pocket)—“can’t do iverything,
an’ that we’re a set o’ chaps ’at may be
talked ower, happen, but willn’t be driven.
Bless ye, Mr. Oliphant, we’d do ought for a
fellow ’at’s kind to us ; but I’ll defy ye, or
ony man alive, ay, or t’ divil hissel, to drive
us ! Well, and we’ve fand out on our side
’at Mr. Oliphant wor an evven-down hard-
hitter, as tough as pinwire and as lish as a
snig—talk about deeing, indeed ! Sae t’ end
on it is ’at it’s a drawn battle an’ we may consider we’ve aw shakked hands an’ are to be
better friends nor iver. What, we’re York-
shiremen, aren’t we, an’ not spiteful Cockneys ? I’ve just come frae amang them

cattle—aa, lord, I sall hev some bonny tales to tell ye about 'em, but I'll put it off a bit, acos Mr. Oliphant there is nobbut sickly yet, an' wants to be back i' his easy chair. Howiver, nebbors, we munnot let him gang wi'out giving him three times three—an' Mr. and Mrs. Howden, too; an' here's a bang-up New Year to 'em aw, an' mony on 'em. Now for it!—Hip—hip—hurrah!"

*   *   *   *   *

More than a year has gone by since the supper, and all the main personages in our story are alive and well, except poor John Hawtrey, who has fallen asleep in the fulness of age and honour, and now lies in the village churchyard, surrounded by none but friends, and overshadowed by the hills he loved. Mr. Oliphant has let Dick Wide-awake have a large farm at a very small rent, and has stocked it for him besides, so that the honest farmer is now a very prosperous man, and, it is even whispered, is not unlikely before long to purchase his old farm of Sandy Topping. He has no time now for horse-jobbing, except, as he says, when he wants a bit of amusement. Tommy Doolittle has also profited by Mr. Oliphant's kindness, and has got the rather valuable post of steward for the Hall estates.

The black sheep of our veracious history, Lord Stainmore—I much wish, for the sake of those readers who love sensation, that nature had made him a villain of deeper dye—has married a great heiress, and lives in splendid style; feeling apparently no twinges except of gout, to which he is occasionally subject, but which his physicians consider due, in his case, rather to an hereditary tendency than to the special retribution that even on earth awaits the sinner, in fiction. Six months ago, Harry

Highside also took to himself a wife, and that wife was no other than the little Italian, Francesca, who had come to the Hall on a long visit, and had grown into an extremely beautiful and lively girl. As usual, Harry surrendered at first sight, and was more fortunate in this than his previous love affairs; for he was successful in his suit, and married her, in spite of a rather strong opposition from Sir George, whom, however, a handsome dower from Mr. Oliphant reconciled in some measure to the match. Fothergill grumbles that it is a great pity such an old family as that of the Highsides should die out, as he says it certainly will now, for Francesca will improve the race so much that there will be no knowing it. He also tells the Holdens that he considers Frank's prosperity a highly immoral thing, and a contradiction of all the eternally established laws of the universe; for Frank's is the only case, he says, in which he ever knew that silly old proverb, about honesty being the best policy, come true in real life. By the bye, these are the only bits of cynicism which William has been known to utter for some months, so wonderfully tame has he grown under Dora's able management.

As for Kate and Frank, they are still at the Hall, permanently settled there, and adored by the whole country side. Kate has given birth to another child, a pretty little daughter ; and Frank has resumed his brush with enthusiasm. Last year, a picture of his in the Academy attracted a good deal of attention, and his artist friends prophesy great things for him. But he wastes so much time in 'chaffing' Kate and playing with the children, or doing kind things generally, that it is quite possible the only fame he may ever achieve will be that of a "ripping good fellow," a title with which the neighbouring squires have already dubbed him.

And Mr. Oliphant? Dear reader, if ever, tempted by the clearness of its river or the beauty of its limestone crags, you wander up our little dale away from the turmoil of earth as far as Reinsber, and then stand on the bridge with its one arch, to watch the streamlet as it flashes and bubbles out its epitomes and satires of human life so prettily, the chances are that, somewhere in the village, you will see a noble-looking old man, erect still, and with that calm, benevolent expression on his features which is always the reflection of a heart at peace with the world and itself. Most likely he will be entering some of the cottages, where he is received with a smile by the goodwife—who dusts the best chair for him at once, as if he were a frequent visitor—

and with shouts of delight by the children, for in his capacious pockets there is generally a store of toys and gingerbread. Or perhaps he will be conversing with some labourer, who is evidently anxious for advice on his little troubles: and the old man's face, as he listens so courteously and kindly, yet so shrewdly, is a study. If you ask any one who the old gentleman is, the answer will probably be, "Ye mun be a stranger, sir, or ye'd knaw Mr. Oliphant; he's a true friend to the poor man, sir, God bless him!" Jabez has parted with all his airs and great schemes, and has become very popular, the carles looking on him as a sort of benevolent uncle, on whose advice and assistance they may in all cases rely. In this way his influence for good, though almost unconsciously exercised, is immense, and he is so satisfied with his present life that the only thing he is sorry for is that he did not come down to Reinsber twenty years before. "But it is no matter," he laughs and says to Kate, "for I shall make up for lost time by living twenty years longer than I intended. I have determined to keep you out of your fortune, Kate, till I am a hundred." And Kate very heartily wishes he may; but tells him there is small chance of his ever reaching a hundred, for at present he is travelling away from it and growing young again.

THE END.

BILLING, PRINTER, GUILDFORD.